TEMPLE
OF THE
DOUBLE SUN

Glenn Lazar Roberts

2025, TWB Press
https://www.twbpress.com

Temple of the Double Sun
Copyright © 2025 by Glenn Lazar Roberts

Edited by Terry Wright

Cover Art by Terry Wright

ISBN: 978-1-959768-89-0

Chapter 1

From some unknown corner of my mind, I became aware of an impulse to awaken, as a shuddering traveled through the hull of *Source*. From some other unknown corner, my mind calmed, reassured the restive child within me that the intense shuddering was predictable, calculated, merely a deceleration from light speed, a slowing that would continue for months more, with its crew, me included, preserved in cryostasis.

The child stopped fretting and returned to sleep, for now, content. But although my ego had reassured my Little One, another impulse from mysterious depths continued to worry, not satisfied with knowing that we colonists from Earth had passed through the first months of acceleration without incident while our craft, christened 'Source,' approached near light speed, hurtling through the immeasurable gulfs of space toward the fortunately named constellation Teknos.

Acceleration, cruising, deceleration. Although I was only an ecologist, and not even the chief ecologist on board, I understood the mechanics well enough, though the theory behind the single quantum jump at the height of our speed escaped me. Wasn't my job.

What I did not understand was why we were allowed to awaken from what seemed an impossibly long cryostatic sleep for a mere three days as the craft reached light speed, then had to rush back into our frozen chambers after the jump as deceleration kicked in.

It was quite a large party. Over two hundred colonists, the people of *Mok-sa* as we call ourselves, of all skills and backgrounds crammed together in a split-level spacecraft with seven women to every man, like a split-level ranch house from southern Utah, a seeming violation of our rule of absolute equality. But all was meticulously planned, all scientifically accounted for in order to most quickly populate the nearest Earth-like planet discovered by the star-gazing Chaldeans back home, whose job it was to ID such things.

With bottles popped and drunk, and the ecstatic shouting over, and many connubial unions consummated, back into the chambers we went, our blood thinned appropriately by a derivative of anti-freeze to enable us to survive the subzero temperature. Our scientists were so advanced that we needed no blood transfusions to awaken for the party, just as we would need none when we finally awoke in our new home.

Our new home.

That's what had us titillated...more than titillated. Happy, enthused, frenetic. Anything might have done this given our relief to escape Earth where the extinction of all edible flesh had forced us a century ago to become Vegans, in our new pacifist language: 'Mok-sa'. But the news of what awaited us on the newly discovered distant planet sent us into orbit. My ego recoiled from the pun; my child smiled.

Smaller than Earth but with less ocean, two-thirds of the surface was one broad continent. First in a series of six planets that circled the double yellow sun we termed *Dimaxia Prime*, such that—as the Chaldeans had declared—its inhabitants would view the two suns merge then partly divagate once per year since all its planets revolved on the same plane as the twin suns. With five variegated moons, the planet's gravity would be almost like Earth's, and although its pole was not slanted like Earth's, the merging and divagating of the suns will provide familiar seasons, and given the thick atmosphere, the poles would not be much colder than the equator.

And perhaps best of all—again as the Chaldeans had assured us—there would be no intelligent life, but only an assortment of native plants and wildlife. There were no human-like inhabitants. No need for guilt due to displacing some soon-to-be civilization of recent tree-dwellers. There were none. Just as there were no signs of intelligent life anywhere on the planet we had named Maalstrom. No buildings, no roads, no farming. The place was clean, as if created for us.

Forty light years away: six months total with three days and one irreversible jump in the middle. Then our new home would open up, and we would breathe its Earth-like atmosphere and spread over its rich fecund surface like happy locusts, free at last from the problems of ancient Earth.

The shuddering rose and fell and finally even my superego calmed and embraced the delicious emptiness. Three voices whispered quietly in the darkness: the child, the man, the scientist.

Are we there yet?

Be patient, Little One. Have faith in a Chaldean Universe.

Chapter 2

W hen I awoke, it was to the bawling of my inner child, as the shuddering increased before it finally ceased.

Quiet.

I calmed him again. It meant only one thing—the endless trip through the void had ended. We had arrived. As the temperatures within the cryostatic chambers rose in response to the microwaved energy pumping by prearrangement into our bodies, I sensed rather than heard chambers creaking open in their long white rows, glimpsed a phalanx of white-clothed passengers emerging from their casings like pale vampires in search of quick infusions of blood. My own chamber opened more slowly, child, ego, and fragile superego returning to where Nature intended them to be, or at least tolerated.

"Something's wrong."

The first voice I heard was our own resident Chaldean, named Yezd, whose close-bearded odd face was, by chance, the first I glimpsed. Through the corner of one eye, I saw his usual cast of careful concern, his one yellow and one blue eye sharpened with worry. His white uniform bore the Greek symbol Omega—our strict protocol of absolute social equality reinforced, in his instance, by placing him last in the hierarchy that scientific enterprises inevitably require, as he was the most learned among us and our only astronomer.

Alpha-1, or Vedega as she was privately known, emerged next to him. "Okay. So the ship is settling at an angle."

Similarly clothed in white, there was no trace of worry on Alpha-1's face despite her observation. She was in command, as the Alpha-1 insignia on her uniform made plain. Perhaps she felt greater responsibility to show calm to bolster the others, she having skipped the wild party scene halfway through the trip. Last in knowledge and training—though still more trained than the average Earth citizen—our protocol had put her in charge for the sake of social stability, a lesson our ancestors had only slowly learned at their cost, given the current state of Old Earth.

Yezd and Vedega headed immediately for the wide door locks gracing one end of Source, the other colonists crowding behind, none taking note of me, the lowly ecologist, Psi-2, of the eight-person Psi unit...next to last in rank, known personally to the others as Milo. Peculiar how my many years of study had steadily reduced me in rank until I was almost an Omega. But that's the sacrifice our society has made in its attempt to reverse the catastrophes. Futile, as it turned out.

A stirring within. *Hush, child. Opinions are not for the likes of us.*

Auto atmosphere testing concluded with a buzz.

"The air is good," Alpha-1 pronounced.

"As I predicted," Yezd Omega said, the only *unit* without a companion, a smug satisfaction showing, as if to disprove his low status as chief of the several mechanically minded eunuchs.

Alpha-1 nodded. "As the astronomers' council on Earth predicted." She subtly corrected him with a casual nod at the engineering team of seven male eunuchs assigned to run the ship under Yezd's direction.

They flicked switches, and a wide brim released an explosion of light, angled, since one end of the ship had sunk six degrees into the earth of Maalstrom, the landing props at one end having sunk into the soft soil of a marsh.

A platform unrolled from beneath the floor. Halfway out, it too became stuck, forcing the excited colonists who spilled out to leap down, ignoring the concerned looks of our engineers and a collection of gnats that instantly rose from the marshy soil. In a rush to be the first to touch the soil of this New Earth, several Mok-sa collided and landed as one.

"Come, Milo," one of the women yelled.

"Are you certain it's safe?" I replied. I felt my own face show more concern than anyone. I stepped down, if not a giant leap, certainly an uncomfortable drop.

The female citizen Psi-3, each Greek letter denoting a single reproductive unit of one male and seven females, grinned at me and pointed at the sky where the clear light of the double suns of Maalstrom streamed down through breaks in thick white clouds. The suns were separating, and assuming Yezd and the council on Earth had been correct, would, before long, appear as two distinct orbs. The Chaldeans were never wrong.

Psi-1, or Bruna as we privately called her, walked swiftly across the grass-strewn dirt, the moisture in the soil that had captured two of the ship's props not enough to inconvenience booted human feet more than half an inch. She kicked a rock, and together we watched it lift and bounce; its arc and skipping demonstrated a gravity indistinguishable from that of Earth.

I said, "Hard to believe this beautiful sunlight only lasts fourteen Earth hours. It will take getting used to. I imagine some of us will remain awake two days straight and then crash on the third."

Bruna nodded agreement. Again, the quick almost-concealed smiles in my direction, especially from my co-wife Psi-4, or Asana. *She's wasting no time getting started,* I thought silently. What will the others in our unit think, especially Vensa Psi-6, who at once threw a reproachful green but violet-eyed glance at me and Asana.

From amidst the crowd of colonists climbing down ladders supplied by the eunuch engineers and gathering on the grassy surface, the women of the Psi unit collected around me, each clothed in a new white worker's uniform. I mentally tagged each one, remembering my training to treat each of my co-wives absolutely equally: Psi-1, or Bruna, our specialist in non-human communication, of course a woman since no man can be the formal head of any unit; Asana Psi-4, highly trained in materials conductivity; Psi-5, or Tumsa, a botanist specializing in tropical adaptations; Vensa Psi-6, our resident biologist; and Psi-7, or Mika, a pharmacologist. Along with Tlata Psi-3, our unit resident psychologist. And how could I forget Morla Psi-8, she of the golden skin and the alluring epicanthic fold possessed by the eunuch engineers, she trained in aeronautics. And I, Milo Psi-2. Eight in total, if we don't count my timorous inner child and defective superego, that is.

I sighed and wondered just how I was going to handle this reproductive thing with seven pairs of eyes spying on me with affected disinterest. With a little relief—or was it schadenfreude?—I saw the other units unconsciously collect around the other twenty-eight men in our colony. Each unit with its own unique combination of specialties, the less challenging ones assigned the prior Greek letters. Twenty-eight men and eight eunuchs in a veritable sea of hyper-fertile women.

Chapter 3

Some distance away, a copse of trees was visible, more copses gradually merging into a dense forest to our south. Green leaves for a yellow sun. Or suns, rather. Tumsa, our Psi unit botanist, could explain the florid greenness better than I.

The engineers unpacked and assembled our only anti-gravity rover and Vedega Alpha-1 stepped inside, accompanied by Nasveta Tau-1 and Sisha Xi-3. The latter was also a biologist like Vensa, though she was not as highly ranked as Nasveta Tau-1. Alpha-1 motioned for me also to step into the rover, and I could not erase the triumphant grin that Little Milo displayed. My child smiled in pride until my glare erased the prideful thought.

The rover could hold a dozen passengers. Vedega, or *Alpha-1*, as I quickly corrected myself, slid the side-door shut, and in another moment we were airborne. Yezd sat at the controls, the ship Source shrinking to the size of a toy as we gained altitude. Then, with the aid of ailerons and rudder, the rover rushed off to commence the first survey of our new home by circling the ship in a spiral pattern. A view-camera transmuted all beneath us into digital storage for later inspection, all done with the rover on auto control while we gazed out the windows, admiring our new home.

All I could see, since our vision was partially blocked by the white clouds, was an endless forest stretching away to the south, and a rocky scarp a mile to our west, nearly hidden by the copse of trees. To the north, grey mountains came into view. To the east, endless high crags enfolding dark valleys with red fires twinkling in their depths.

"There is nothing at our current location to shelter the ship," Alpha-1 pronounced. "It would be better if we could move it to those trees for the shade."

Sisha, Nasveta, and I nodded. It was best not to contradict Vedega, though Nasveta, I mean *Tau-1*, and I were trained in ecology whereas Vedega's only training was *stage management*. Not formally correct, but that was how I thought of her leadership training, though I dared think such thoughts only to myself, just as I dared speak of her only as *Alpha-1*, out of respect for our leader.

In half an hour, the rover was back at Source and landed gently by the front gate of the ship, taking care not to sink also into the soft wet ground. The engineers had opened the gate further, and the other 224 colonists had begun setting up facilities for our biological functioning.

"Can't wait to taste the first fruits of Maalstrom," Lamoc Rho-3 called, grinning as he approached. He was my closest friend among the men. His short black beard attracted admiring stares from women of more than one unit.

Don't be jealous, Little One. We'll have plenty to keep us busy every evening.

The insignia of Rho-3 was visible on Lamoc's white suit, all of us displaying our own similar insignia on our crisp new uniforms.

"Deciduous plant growth," I said, "extending west and south. North...difficult. East? Well, no one will want to go there."

Lamoc nodded, as if acknowledging my superior training. Unlike some, he always ignored my low rank. A friend.

"The rover's cameras caught some bright colors in the forests," I added. "I'll bet that's edible fruit."

Lamoc grinned again. Then two of his unit's women took him by the arms and led him away, flashing smiles.

Alpha-1 was hobnobbing with Yezd. From twenty feet off, I saw the two of them staring at the ship's marsh-entangled props and Yezd shaking his head.

That was clear enough. We were marooned. Not that we had any intention to return to Earth or even the ability. The quantum jump could not be reversed and Source had been supplied on Earth with only enough energy to bring us to our new planet.

Our commander swung her arms to wave off gnats and yelled to gain the attention of the crew. "We're going to move to that oasis over there." She pointed to the distant copse of trees by the escarpment. "Our survey shows ample shade and water and plenty of nitrogen in the soil. We can plant our first crop." Alpha-1 broke a sincere smile, and the rest of us followed suit. Raising her face to the sky, she uttered the ancient formula as the others listened silently: "May it be good, fortunate, propitious." With that, the crew began loading facilities into the rover for transport to the distant trees.

It was the end of our first day on Maalstrom, and we had already constructed much of our first barracks and begun installing privacy walls for the women. Yezd flew the rover back and forth, tirelessly, until all the materials we required had found a place in the barracks while the eunuchs organized its further construction.

I helped by supervising the organization of the common eating area and helping to install the water container and refrigerators for our food while the engineers installed the wiring. Not that we had ample electricity, only a small generator capable of powering the refrigerators. Our plan was to rough it like pioneers. Since we had to hoard our power, night lights in our barracks would come from primitive oil lamps.

Once the common area was built, I inspected it in detail, and accompanied by several women, cleaned the tables and the new hard glass windows the engineers had installed, all the while swatting at pests which I tossed into the trash receptacle behind the refrigerators, including what looked like moths and mayflies. I have ever been a stickler for cleanliness. Perhaps it comes with the title ecologist. I then joined the remainder of the men who were planting the first seedlings of wheat in the new fields while the women helped the engineers set up the communal barracks.

Chapter 4

I still remember my first inkling that things were out of sort more seriously than props stuck in mud.

Vensa Psi-6 disappeared, my unit's resident biologist, and—dare I think it?—my favorite Psi unit 'partner'. It happened only two weeks after the barracks had been built and ditches constructed around the spring to direct a flow of water to the newly planted fields. One day Vensa was in the new barracks in her private quarters. The next day she was gone.

Intensive searches of our new town, which we christened *Klopus* for the common wheat called *Klopan* that we had sown, failed to locate her. Yezd even flew the rover in another wide search pattern. Without result. She was not just the Psi unit's best biologist, but, as she was lowest in rank, she was therefore the best biologist the colony had.

When Yezd returned, he reminded Alpha-1 that the rover's energy packs were limited and that Source could only recharge them a few times before the rover would become useless.

We were not concerned about mere machines, however. We only wanted to know what had happened to our friend Vensa. I already missed her violet eyes, having mated with her in the privacy of her room multiple times in the first two weeks, in addition to during our three-day party while in flight, the only partner I had had an interest in.

"You are so exciting," she had exclaimed. "But the others are jealous."

"Don't be concerned, my beloved Vensa. They will follow their duty." Her ecstatic smile—she had seemed to enjoy our mating more than I would have thought—turned into a frown at my comment.

Like everyone on the crew, we had only been introduced to our own unit just before we entered Source and I had not seen any sign of jealousy at the time, just as I had failed to see how mating could be of more interest to anyone than the impact of cloned Klopan wheat on the various minuscule rodent species that we soon identified to match the insects I began to collect. But what can I say? When it comes to women...

Then our best ecologist, Nasveta Tau-1, took sick and confined herself to her room, refusing entry to her mate Tau-3, or Khurko, who became increasingly abrasive, she even refusing to allow Alpha-1, or the ship's medical doctor Sigma-1, to enter, or even to allow the doctor to peer through the outer window which Nasveta covered with black cloth. We had been so confident of our perfect genetics that to include more than one medical doctor had been omitted as needless.

"Mutiny," Alpha-1 muttered under her breath by Nasveta's door while I peered from behind, straining to see what was the matter with another of the colony's women.

"What do you think, Milo?" Alpha-1 asked me.

"Nasveta is competent, and she is her unit leader. I think you should give her time." I was glad that Nasveta's male, Khurko Tau-3, stood alongside and heard my encouragement. He showed no sign of appreciation but only glared.

Alpha-1 nodded. We were all emotionally strained with the stresses of our colonization and apparently even Alpha-1, as it turned out, had an empathetic side, to my surprise.

However, I was not overly worried, as the colonization was proceeding exceedingly well, all our needs were rapidly met by our engineer eunuchs and the capable skills of over two hundred carefully selected and trained, young and hardy colonists. Yezd and his eunuchs even began assembling an old-fashioned helicopter we had brought for the time when Source's power packs would be exhausted and the rover's gravity-neutralizer no longer work. The helicopter's electric battery required less energy than the rover's dense power packs. I believe this was more hobby than necessity. How else should one expect engineers to occupy themselves after Klopus was fully built and humming, and Source abandoned, than constructing something?

Then Nasveta vanished.

The mystery was now more than concerning. Losing one fertile female was statistically likely. Losing two within a month unlikely. And when two more women of other units locked themselves in their private rooms, the entire colony began to worry. At least—as I reassured paranoiac Little Milo—different units meant it could not be due to something *I* had done. The infection—I hesitated over the word, but what else could it be—had spread to other units whose women were mating exclusively with other males according to our strict scientific protocol to avoid conflict and in-breeding. So, it could not be any fault of mine. But still I missed Vensa's veiled violet eyes and Nasveta's compulsion to discuss ecology with me despite her mate Khurko's frowns, Nasveta and I being the only ecologists.

The women's absence depressed me.

Chapter 5

Another two weeks passed and the isolated women among the other units still had not emerged when, one evening, Lamoc again approached me, beneath a green blanket cast by Maalstrom's largest moon.

Glancing to left and right, standing beside a gurgling culvert bathed in lurid green shadows, Lamoc Rho-3 sidled closer and whispered, "Have you heard, Milo?"

"Heard? Heard what?" Lamoc had more of that mysterious thing called congeniality than I possessed, and women from other units often spoke to him of things they would never say to me.

Again the sidelong glance, though no one was near, almost the entire colony at this late hour ensconced in the barracks. He whispered: "She gave birth. It was *deformed*."

I was shocked. All of us crew had been carefully selected not just for top physical health but for the health of our DNA going back several generations. Our genetics were free from defect, and our immunities the best. As an ecologist, if not a geneticist, I knew that a deformed birth was impossible among us.

"But how?" I stared at Lamoc through the green rays with incredulity. "That cannot be."

"It can. And it is."

I was still skeptical. "Did you see the infant yourself?"

He shook his head. "Vedega did...I mean, Alpha-1. At least, that's what I heard from a woman in the Pi unit. And they are very high in rank."

Little Milo let loose a wry smile, more schadenfreude. "Doesn't mean a thing. You know what Pis know...next to nothing."

Lamoc's eyes grew wide at my impious remark. He stared askance again as if spies were listening. "Mutinous talk, Milo. Because you are my friend, I will forget I heard that."

I backtracked. "I mean, even their advanced rank must require them to see such impossible evidence with their own eyes before making such a claim."

"Alpha-1 isn't enough of a witness?"

"If she saw it herself, but you cannot verify that Alpha-1 saw anything."

"True..." Lamoc's voice trailed off. He was too busy watching for eavesdroppers to pay further attention. He nodded then hurried away to vanish in the sea of mottled green.

The next day Klopus was abuzz with the usual obsessing over our quick-growing crop of Klopan when the first indigenous animals were sighted, apart from the predictable assortment of rodents and insects, most of the latter being the swamp gnats and a few cautious hornets and moths. As vegans, we crew of the Source refrained from meat of all sorts and had brought no animals such as our ancestors had once eaten. Earth had no more domestic animals anyway; whatever was edible had long been eaten into extinction.

I was invited to go on an expedition with several females of another unit and their male, all Mues. I had not yet learned any of their names. Already bored with watching crops grow, I managed to press myself into their service.

We hiked across the sparsely treed landscape stretching to the west of Klopus to explore the denser forest, and here we encountered a wide, slowly moving river headed in its own purposeful way to the distant southern sea that Yezd asserted lay beyond the rover's highest concentric circle.

Hardly had we arrived at the northeast bank of the lazy river than the surface of the water was broken by a trio of sinuous grey necks; at the end of each curled a narrow fish-like head. Three pairs of wide, moist eyes stared at us in surprise and incomprehension. We stood still, not wanting to frighten them, not any more than we ourselves were frightened, I should say. Old picture-book images of extinct Earth crocodiles sprang to my mind. However, in another moment the animals rushed to the far shore and clambered onto the bank to expose barrel-like bodies and four limbs, aided in their climb by claw-equipped feet. Gills on the sides of their narrow heads glistened with streaming water.

"Huh," I remarked. "Amphibians. Wild amphibians, and fish-eaters from the looks of their needle-like teeth."

The animals disappeared into the brush.

The others relaxed. Gathering plant and insect samples, we returned to Klopus. Too bad we had brought no cameras; we were already reverting to a medieval-like lifestyle. We had only our word to bring back, like Alpha-1's upon allegedly finding a deformed birth in someone's private quarters.

Two more weeks passed. To everyone's surprise but mine, several more female crew members isolated themselves. It seemed that the more our males performed their reproductive duties, the more women absented themselves. What for? I morosely felt that the full connotations of the...*infection* would soon arrive.

Morning came brightly, the double suns still in the process of divagating, their summer rays springing crops and forest greenery from their energy with inexorable force.

Looking up, I saw the crew rushing to the barracks where some commotion was occurring. I hurried too. At the entrance stood Alpha-1, with Yezd, and the entire Pi unit which I perceived at once had suffered some terrible blow.

Alpha-1 bellowed—a deep tone I had thought her incapable of. *Must be her stage training,* I elbowed Little Milo. "Everyone assemble," Alpha-1 yelled. "Bad news."

I squeegeed through the crowd. I wanted verification this time, not hearsay.

Her pretty features with her blue eyes gleaming as she spoke (I could not help myself: my hormones were at full flood as I fulfilled my drone-like duties among the women each night. Might she even join my Psi unit? I fantasized.) "There's been a death."

Immediately I expected the obvious, that one of the secluded women had died, perhaps in childbirth, which was also exponentially unlikely. Instead, Alpha-1 surprised me: "Telemer, the male of the Pi unit has taken his own life."

I caught my breath. *Suicide?* That was as unlikely as deformed births.

Taking a breath, Alpha-1 resumed: "We found him dead in his unit quarters. There is no indication that anyone else was involved. He shot himself with an old-fashioned pistol, an heirloom he had brought. Against protocol, I might add."

Shot himself? I was more than stunned. That was impossible. As impossible as everything else that was happening to us.

Slowly, amid a buzz of conversation, the crew dispersed, and Alpha-1 and several engineers entered the Pi unit and brought the male's body out, which they carried to the field the next day to provide extra fertilization for our Klopan crop. Contrary to ancient heroic ages, we Mok-sa no longer burned our dead, but let them decompose gradually in shallow soil as Nature intended. We had scientifically replaced cemeteries with verdant fields of agriculture. It was the fondest wish of all Mok-sa that our bodies be returned to the soil to nourish future generations.

I repeated the word 'Nature' to myself. Could there be a Nature on alien planets that was not what we had expected? Something that might surprise even an ecologist?

More days passed and Lamoc came up to me while I stood meditating one night, contemplating the several moons with melancholy, the land now bathed by the faint red glare of a smaller moon. Lamoc lurked as if avoiding more eavesdroppers. Khurko Tau-3 stood behind him, laying a surly glare upon me. I could not forget that he had been Nasveta's mate, the other ecologist whom I had enjoyed talking with and who had now vanished.

Lamoc leaned in. "What did I tell you, Milo?"

"Why, what do you mean, Lamoc?"

"About the deformed births," he hissed.

"I have seen no deformed births. I think you are imagining that."

It was his turn to look skeptical. "Well, why do you think the Pi male shot himself?"

I shrugged. "A defect in his DNA. That can happen to anyone."

He shook his head. "No, Milo. He was the male from Pi. He was the father of...*you know what*. He *saw* the births. Keep this under your cap, but it was one of the Pi females who informed me of what was happening among them. Two Pi women had given birth to..." he glanced around again surreptitiously, "monstrosities."

"Not enough time," I laughed. "Takes nine months, you fool."

"Not in this case. It was fast, deadly fast. They gave birth in the presence of the other Pi females. In just six weeks. When they saw what had happened, they swore each other to silence." He glanced about. "But one told me anyway."

"Why don't you tell Alpha-1? She is in command. She can do something."

"Oh, she did something alright." He grunted. "She and the engineers crushed the things that the diseased Pi women had given birth to."

Now I was truly shocked. "How could they legally do that? Such acts require informing the entire crew and obtaining the consent of everyone beforehand." With an effort, I asked the inevitable: "*What* did they give birth to?"

He blinked. "Eggs. Small white eggs."

Khurko leveled a hard gaze on Lamoc and Lamoc ceased speaking. Throwing a last hostile glare at me, Khurko sloughed away in silence with Lamoc in tow.

From somewhere, an insect, the kind I had seen commonly in the Klopan oasis and in the forest to the south, circled near. I waved the hornet away while thanking the gods Maalstrom had no mosquitos or we would really be in trouble.

Chapter 6

The next morning, we first glimpsed an... *apparition*. A single speck high above the horizon, at first mistaken for a bird, of which we had already identified several species, all harmless. But as it flew, or rather glided closer, the entire crew erupted from our barracks to view *what could not be*. Closer it drifted and descended to circle our little settlement with shining baleful eyes to rid us of our—innocent?—illusion that we were alone. In the midst of the crowd of my fellow peaceful Mok-sa, I felt them catch their breath.

Aloft on two bat-like leathern wings, the creature was humanoid with two arms suspended below and two human-like legs trailing behind. The head and torso were of the sort to inhabit our nightmares...or should I say dreams? The body, which was first to acquire precise form, was that of a female Mok, a human-like woman, endowed by whatever its Creator may have been, with pendulous breasts, narrow waist, and the hips of a female in reproductive prime as *she*—and how could I think of it otherwise given her charms—

descended to less than a dozen meters above us where it seemed to contemplate the fate of the soil-bound things below. Her two breasts were crowned with hard nipples. Her smooth face with its two bright fair eyes was framed by an ample flag of blond hair flitting in the breeze, and her perfect full lips rippled open then closed as if she had thought to speak but decided at the last moment against it. Perhaps most stunning of all—if anything could be more stunning than the sudden appearance of such an apparition on what we had imagined a planet free of intelligent life—was a plain brown cloth tied with a simple rope encompassing her abdomen to hide the last proof of gender. No animal weaves cloth.

I never heard a silence so complete. No one moved a finger. That simple brown cloth was indisputable proof that intelligent life existed on this supposedly empty planet.

As my mind, in a tangle with panicked Little Milo, clutched spasmodically to make connections between births, the suicide, and our vanished women, and utterly failing, I watched the thing circle once, twice, then as if following a scent, rocket toward the fields of Klopan wheat where it alighted beside the corpse of the Pi male who lay peacefully between foot-wide rows in preparation for a shallow burial later today.

Rushing toward the fields to get a better view, the crowd slowed as we neared the creature. Astonished, I saw it lift the corpse in its two arms, which were clearly far stronger than I had given them credit for, and launch itself into the sky with its burden. Within minutes it disappeared over the southwest horizon.

I don't believe a word was said the rest of that fateful day. Not by me. Not by Alpha-1. Not even by Yezd who stood in the yard and stared at the sky for hours until the rushing moons gathered above Maalstrom.

Seeing me that evening, Lamoc kept to himself, Khurko glowering by his side, chewing, ever chewing.

The silence of my fellow Mok-sa continued through the evening and into the next day. They turned to their usual tasks, habit overcoming horror, and most resumed their planting duties, occasionally taking breaks for a repast or to couple with a unit mate.

For the next week, no other apparitions appeared in the sky, which at times was clear as a church bell, at others swept by leaden clouds hurrying in from the distant southern sea to spill their burden before the rocky range to our north, refreshing our fields with lifegiving water.

The Rho unit announced a pregnancy. Any

other time such would have been an occasion for rejoicing; we would soon parent a prosperous population as we Mok-sa spread out across the landscape of towns and rich crop-crowned fields shining golden beneath the glorious double sun.

Not now.

I sensed a new firmness among our leaders, a guardedness as if conscious of menace. Alpha-1 stopped smiling. I buried her personal name, Vedega, as I found myself caught up in the new collective resolve, and for once I was glad we had a strong leader.

Her unit male, Alpha-8 (the higher the Greek letters, the lower the rank allowed to their subservient male) alone seemed happy. I glimpsed him late evening hobnobbing with Lamoc and two of his female Alpha paramours. *He is fortunate.* Who would not consider himself fortunate to mate regularly with such a magnificent female like Alpha-1, not to mention the rest of his highly ranked females. Even from across the barracks deck, I could see him flex and motion with his arms, expressing his vigor, the red cloak of Maalstrom's red moon broaching the horizon as the short day of fourteen Earth hours came to a close, and some headed for sleep while others sought to remain awake, planning to sleep the second night.

Another week passed, and I had a chance to

overhear Alpha-1 and Yezd exchange more words around a corner of the barracks. Their tone was serious.

"I still say we should take the rover," Alpha-1 said. "The thing must have come to ground not far away. It flew to the southwest."

Yezd shook his head. "The batteries are sufficient, yes, but what if we should need the rover for a future emergency?"

She stared, puzzled. "Like what? Isn't it best to survey the wildlife, the better to avoid future emergencies?"

"Source is sinking farther into the ground with each week. Our attempts to dislodge its props have used much power. We can no longer fully recharge the rover once the current power packs are spent."

She frowned. "You assured me it would work this time, Yezd, that you could get the ship loose."

He shrugged. "I was wrong. Source is spent and useless." He scanned the moonlit sky as if the *thing* might reappear. He took a breath. "I have a name for it."

"A name? Names are sacred, Yezd. You know they carry significance deep into one's soul."

Making an innocuous shake of his head, he said, "We could call it a *malkop*. In our Mok-sa language: *Maalstrom-vulture*."

"That alludes to its strange interest in our

corpse." She sighed. "It seems appropriate."

Thus, we came to embrace a name for the apparition that had visited us and thrown us into such confusion.

Another week passed, and three unit males collected on the barrack's landing after the day's labors were done, doubtless to share their pleasure in fertilizing so many attractive young females. Such public demonstration was something I myself was loath to do, though I confess I too was experiencing a certain elation from my own drone-like duties.

From the corner of my eye, I saw the male from the Rho unit burst excitedly from the barracks.

"It's happened. It happened again. In the Upsilon unit."

Dragged along by the rush of males into the barracks, I barreled to the Upsilon unit rooms. The door to one of the females was locked shut.

"I saw her. I saw *it*," the Upsilon male yelled, then exploded into tears. With a crash, he broke down the locked wooden door and we pressed into the private quarters of Upsilon-2, her personal name unknown to me.

The Upsilon female screamed, tried to cover up the product of her birth. The Upsilon male snatched the cover away and we recoiled at what, again, was impossible.

Lamoc had been correct. As we stood there beneath the mad moons on this alien planet, their varied lunar colors playing about the open windows, our eyes peered at a shining white oval: an egg.

I wretched and sprang out. Others hurried in, group after group until the entire crew must have seen it.

Now Alpha-1 came, followed by our Chaldean. Imperiously, she yanked the cover away. At a glance from Yezd as if they had prearranged something, she declared, "Do not kill it. We shall nurse it and see what develops."

Outside in the hallway, I could hardly believe what I had just heard. *Destroy it*, I thought. *Smash it*, added Little Milo, *before it's too late*.

But they did not.

Under Alpha-1's order and observed by a pair of stern strong females posted permanently at the Upsilon-woman's door, both the male and the mother were restrained and barred from entering while a series of technicians inspected the egg.

Since Vensa, our top-ranked ecologist, had long since vanished, the job of top ecologist fell onto my reluctant shoulders, and after our chief medical doctor located a feeding aperture in the already-squirming egg, I was led in to examine it and give my own pronouncement.

With renewed shudders I watched two women feed the thing a mixture of sugar and water through its dark-lipped aperture, and I leaned over to see what I could. Nothing in my training had prepared me for such. It let loose a distinct mewing as if already conscious that this would trigger more feeding. The women squirted more sugar water into the orifice...I could not bring myself to call it a mouth.

I shuddered. Turned to Alpha-1. "I have no clue. Who knows how it came to be? Or what it means?"

Frowning, she ordered me out.

More time passed. It seemed an enormous span of time. However, I was only too aware that mere days were passing. Little Milo had lapsed into a catatonic state, even more unwilling to contemplate our bleak future than I.

Three weeks passed... Four weeks, keeping in mind the short Maalstrom day of only fourteen hours, the double suns hurrying on their swift errand only to be as swiftly followed by the five variegated moons. It was far too short a time for anything human to develop from the *thing*, as I could only think of it.

Yet it grew.

When less than a week had passed, I was called in again to inspect and was shocked to discover that it had already matured into what could only be called a pupa in the shape of a purplish-white lozenge. The mouth was now distinct, and human-like teeth were visible as it opened its jaws for its accustomed nourishment. Its mewling had changed to a crying hardly distinguishable from a Mok-sa human infant.

What devilish plot had seized us? With an angry outburst, I yelled, "Kill it. Or we shall all regret what comes forth."

The women looked not at it with horror, but at *me*, as if I had voiced some sacrilege. They returned to their feeding, injecting vast quantities of sugary water now mixed with human milk derived from our powdered stocks intended to nourish a large generation of Mok-sa children.

I stalked out as Alpha-1 reentered to establish order, and Yezd followed behind where he stood and stared.

Need I relate what happened further once the thing matured in a mere three weeks more? Little Milo knows. We all know.

The day came when the lozenge had grown to a full three feet in length and weighed at least fifteen pounds. By this time more eggs had appeared among us; they too were rapidly gaining weight as they consumed further stocks of our scarce powdered milk and the milky expressions of their own biological mothers. Many of our males reacted with horror and refused any further mating, terrified of the consequences. Several more of our women disappeared. Others barred their doors to all and everyone. Our most expertly trained scientists analyzed and investigated and sifted and tested but came up with no explanation, or prognosis.

I tried to remain far from the barracks entrance, even avoiding speaking with Lamoc, whom I unreasonably partly blamed for the catastrophe. Yet not so distant that I could not hear if anything was amiss.

That morning, I heard another great cry rise among our crew, and turning my head, saw a crowd gather about the entrance and file inside.

I could not help myself. I too rushed in to see what further evil had developed. Inside, I squeezed through and managed to peer over a host of shoulders into the guarded room. The lozenge had torn. The dry husk lay on the wooden-planked floor and its former occupant stretched two pale legs to stand upright and bend two pale arms once, twice. It shook its humanoid head, letting a mop of loose blond hair tousle and flick. A pair of still delicate, almost transparent wings of taut skin stretched out to a width of six feet, causing our people to lurch back as if in the presence of El

Diablo himself. But it was not male. Although less than two months old by Earth standards, the thing was already decked with human-like breasts and a narrow waist. The face was more than familiar—it seemed a perfect copy of what we had seen months earlier in the sky—the thing that had seized the body of the Upsilon male and transported it to...who knew where?

"A malkop." I was the first to blurt it out.

Yezd stared with rippling lips; Alpha-1 with wide eyes.

More cries resounded from the entrance, and we all rushed outdoors where we halted. Several pointed skyward. In the heavens, circling while staring haughtily down upon us, were three more of the creatures, as fully grown as had been the other visitor, each the size of an average Mok woman and as beautiful in appearance, their abdomens fully covered as before.

Something clicked. I stalked back to the malkop that we had nursed and protected. I had not noticed at first shock; now I peered in order to nail it into my memory. Pushing aside one of the female guards, I stared between the thing's legs. The thing had a sex...it was female.

Chapter 7

By this time, the repeated efforts of Yezd and his engineers to dislodge Source from the mud had drained the ship's energy stores and Alpha-1 ordered the rover charged one last time, what was left from Source going into the battery of the now valuable helicopter the engineers had built. Did I detect a hint of desperation in Alpha-1's orders? We had hoped not to be reduced to a medieval economy quite so soon.

Perhaps this, even more than the appearance of a young malkop among us, triggered the next event: Vedega Alpha-1, at the insistent urging of the males who had not chosen self-immolation, forced her way into the chamber where the malkop grew, the unsmiling men pressing behind. The thing's nurturers were ordered to leave, and the thing's mother was dragged out amidst her tearful cries.

The males pushed past Alpha-1 to the malkop. I followed.

Her malkop wings were already taut and brown, no longer translucent, the color due to brown feathery hairs. Her blond hair had blossomed into a lustrous yellow. Her muscles had developed on her legs and above all on the backs of her shoulder blades, where she repeatedly flapped and tested her wings. I dove beneath a wing and slammed shut the wide-open windows at her back for fear she may already be capable of leaping through and taking to air.

The Omicron male extracted a large blade and pointed it at the malkop. "Thus to all enemies of us Mok-sa," he hissed.

Yezd squeezed late into the small room, joined by Alpha-1, who stepped back with anger on her face. But our leader said nothing.

To my surprise, the malkop showed what could only be fear: her eyes widened, she sucked a breath and tensed. How could a virtual newborn comprehend the threat of death? I wondered. Yet she made no noise; her all-too-human mouth twisted as if attempting to protest, but made no sound. I concluded that just as we had heard nothing from the creatures above, and nothing now when the malkop felt extinction coming, that they were mute.

The dagger plunged.

Still no human sound resulted, except for a bizarre clicking like that of a cicada. She slumped and a gush of red blood spilled onto the rough wood floor.

I turned away. Murder is not pleasant—even the murder of an alien that one believes an enemy. Slowly, disconsolately on the part of Alpha-1 as I was certain, we filed out as the engineers dragged the body on a small rug woven of Klopan-fiber and carried it out.

What does one do with the corpse of an insect-like humanoid? Our custom of course was to allow all carbon-based life forms to decompose in our sacred fields once we had consecrated their spiritual essences to our rational god Teknos, in whose constellation our new planet, Maalstrom, resided. In preparation for this, the engineers carried the dead malkop onto the wooden landing that served as our primary social gathering patio when not in the common eating room in the barracks.

By what was now habit, we scanned the skies and immediately sighted the three full-grown malkops we had earlier seen. We had been a crowd, but as the malkops rushed down upon us with harsh glares, the crowd scattered, and I am not ashamed to admit I did likewise. Even the phlegmatic eunuchs, usually imperturbable, dropped their load and ran inside the barracks, perhaps valuing their genetics even more than knowing that their own would not continue in the new world we were founding.

To our amazement, one of the malkops descended and hovered directly over the patio where it stared upon us as if in warning. Watching from within the door, I could swear the other malkops spilled tears down their beautiful pale cheeks. The first alighted, and before any of us could react, it snatched the corpse of the newborn malkop and launched into the sky.

In moments their forms melded into the far southwest horizon.

We had little time to contemplate. That very evening, the twenty surviving males organized a search party, and arming themselves with daggers and clubs, began a search of every room in the barracks. I sat in the field, silencing Little Milo with my hands over my ears as the barracks erupted in screams and shouts, and flames burst from several windows. In short order another half-dozen eggs, pupae, and one just-born malkop were dragged from the women's rooms amid shrieks and screams, assembled into a rough pile, and once drenched with flammables, erupted in a ghastly bonfire. I can still hear the horrid clicking of the little one torn from life so brutally.

At least no grown malkops came to rescue her. Adding that to my list of ecological knowledge, I concluded that the creatures only fly in daytime, which, to me, made them seem even more human-like.

How could we do such deeds? Where was our vaunted rationality, our pride in logic and scientific social order? Could we still call ourselves Mok-sa? If we were no longer Mok-sa, what were we becoming? Of what use would our knowledge and science be if we became something else?

The next day, Lamoc approached me, again accompanied by surly Khurko Tau-3, leader of the lynch mob males, who was still chewing on something secret. Lamoc had a harder look about him than before.

With some effort I managed to fix his angry gaze. "How could you, Lamoc? Who gave you permission to do such?"

He pointed rudely at me. "We are under siege, Milo. Haven't you got that? It's the windows. Our women left open their windows, and some infection drifted in and created this catastrophe." He glanced at the barracks where a commotion of hammering could be heard. "We are closing them all. Permanently."

Khurko Tau-3 spat out between his evil consumption of what I discovered with a shock to be some kind of animal flesh. "We will burn this out with flames," he said.

Feebly I responded, "It may help. You can't be sure."

Glenn Lazar Roberts

"What else can we do?" Lamoc scanned the sky again, his companions balling their hands nervously into fists while one held a scythe, newly sharpened. "We will stamp this infection out before it spreads."

"It has already spread."

"Spreads further."

"And if you fail?"

"Well, we must do something."

I breathed deep. "How many did you kill last night?"

They exchanged guilty stares. "You saw. One malkop. And a batch of eggs and a pupa."

I let it out. "I mean how many *Mok-sa*?"

Their glances looked guiltier. "What does it matter? Any woman who tries to defend the diseased product of her labor we shall cut down. And any man who dares interfere with our eradication effort will be cut down too. The entire colony is at stake."

"How *many*?" I repeated.

"Six Mok-sa. Including one deranged male attempting to defend his diseased females."

With a sigh, I looked sadly at him.

The blade extended again. Lamoc stepped closer, his look harder. "We need every male to own up, Milo. There are only twenty-one of us left."

"And less than one hundred ninety women left

to colonize a planet," I shot back.

Lamoc stared harder. "There can be no middle ground here, Milo. We may have to do this again. We will need your help. Are you with us?"

"Maybe I can best serve by continuing to analyze the problem to find the cause."

He spat on the ground. "That is for the likes of Yezd and his eunuchs. Not *true* men." The four displayed knowing smirks among themselves, and with a nod from Lamoc they moved away.

"Lamoc," I called.

They paused.

"Where was Alpha-1 in all that? Did she give the order for what you did?"

Puzzlement settled. "Didn't you know? Alpha-1 vanished yesterday. We saw Vedega walking across the fields as we made our plans. No one has seen her since. Good riddance. We are purging Klopus of all weakness. If she dares return, we shall deal with her too."

So there has been a coup.

Another thought perturbed. After the other males had left, I walked casually around the entire wide barracks and its two extensions to where the rover and the helicopter rested. With some relief I confirmed that the two flying vehicles remained in place on a field of crushed stone. I watched two engineers stroll nonchalantly about. I wasn't fooled.

Who gave the order for that? Could Yezd have posted them after witnessing Alpha-1's weak acquiescence to the lynch mob? I had not seen our engineers guard anything before this.

Back in my rooms, I did not know what to think, what to feel, what to do. When what remained of my unit women approached me, after the disappearance of Vensa, Nature took over and I found myself in private with Morla Psi-8, she of the golden skin and epicanthic fold. For some reason I found her features more erotic than ever and performed what even the little one within me applauded as an admirable job of fertilization, and at length, I collapsed in her arms as we shared labored breaths in her small room half-lit by one of the old-fashioned oil lamps that the engineers had provided with vegetable oil in order to prevent draining our shrinking power supply.

Despite the chaos and rumors swirling about the colony, my women remained enthusiastic as ever in our mating—I paused at my use of this ancient and supposedly eradicated thought of masculine possession: *my women*—but when in the throes of passion, I found I could not control my thoughts. During the act of creation, like some genetic atavism, I felt I owned each woman of my unit, those Enlightened who planned our colony sensibly assigning each woman to only one male to avert social chaos. Yes, we males were drones, but not without influence. And given the lynch mob's new harsh order, we were all becoming something more. More atavism? Apparently, the Chaldeans and the other planners back on Earth had failed to account for something fundamental within the men, something that had reappeared now that the colony was threatened.

Coming out of my reverie, I gave a powerful kiss to Morla and exited to recharge my body in the communal area. Walking past Bruna's door, I noticed that her back window was open a crack, despite the wooden boards that Khurko and Lamoc had ordered installed throughout the colony. It was not Bruna's turn with me until the following evening, but I felt impelled to plug the crack to seal the window.

Bruna smiled up at me sweetly and I smiled back. At that moment, through the crack, a small hornet of green and iridescent flame, an insect we had termed a *leroo* after capturing a specimen near the river, flew in. It settled on Bruna's arm and thrust. Surprisingly, she did not react but continued to eye me with a gentle smile. Leaning over her—she caught her breath as if anticipating unscheduled love-making—I crushed the insect.

Bruna glanced down in surprise.

A tiny welt had appeared.

"It stung you."

"Oh?" she shook her strawberry blond head and shrugged.

Worried even more than usual, I left. She had not noticed the sting.

Outside, I ate a vegetable repast while I stood in the swirling shadows of the moon-haunted evening. My mind kept coming back to the leroo hornet. Why had she not felt it when it stung her? Could others have been stung, perhaps while they slept? The welt was so small it could be easily overlooked. For weeks our windows had been kept open to enjoy the night air. On a planet devoid of mosquitos, we had paid little attention to its insects aside from collecting a few odd specimens, giving full faith to our genetics and immunities.

Chapter 8

Another week hurried past and the crops of Klopan wheat grew swiftly beneath the twin suns in our widely sown fields. I did my best to banish my worries, most of all what fate might lie in wait for the women of my unit, who perhaps, despite themselves, would not refrain from mating with me whatever may ensue. Although we had only first met before Source launched on its journey, I cared for my women, wanted them to be happy, wanted to see the children of their labors running about, their future—my future. Not one normal Mok baby had yet been born, however, though of course that would require the equivalent of nine Earth months, and we had only been on Maalstrom for three. So far not even a sign...

Within a few days came a repeat of the earlier chaos. Panicked by the defection of Vedega Alpha-1, Khurko Tau-3 and Lamoc Rho-3 recruited fifteen men and once again ransacked the barracks. With the assistance of two hesitant engineers, they had milled several old-fashioned rifles and now they burst into room after room, and before long reemerged with a Mok woman and her male with more eggs in tow. Thank the gods she was not of my unit for I would have felt urged to intervene just as this desperate male must have done. I was too much of a coward to intervene. Behind them, women threw themselves on the patio, and to my amazement, pled for their monstrous eggs to be returned.

Khurko ordered the man and woman to stand on the edge of the planks. The men holding the rifles aimed at the hapless couple.

"No mercy," Khurko shouted. "This is how animals deal with animals. And that is what we are."

I puzzled at this blasphemy, which was something no rational Mok could ever utter. But I clapped my hands to my ears as several earth-shattering explosions sent the doomed couple crashing to the dirt in a bloody ruin.

"You know what to do," Khurko called to the rest of his lynch mob.

Unceremoniously, they dragged the bodies across the intervening fields to a distant windrow where they attempted to cover them with dirt, but soon abandoned this and returned to the barracks, eyeing the skies with concern.

For good reason.

Within a half hour they came—a dozen of the

creatures as if they now knew where to find their favorite prey. As dusk settled, its shadow-line racing across the ground like a sparrow, Khurko jumped into the fields and let loose a rifle shot.

It missed. But with the report, the malkops jerked and flew upward where, after a minute, as if debating what to do, they relented and flew again southwest. I was almost glad his shot had missed. Who knew what the consequences might have been if an other-worldly interloper murdered a malkop that was native to Maalstrom?

Wondering also whether we had successfully reasserted ourselves in the face of the threat with something so simple as a loud noise, the next day I walked into the fields, along with several other Mok-sa, and saw what I expected. The bodies of the executed man and woman were gone. The creatures had come in the night. At this, I halted to wrestle again with my thoughts. How often had they visited us when we slept? For months our broad windows had been innocently left open...

Another short week, and in the midst of my mating, I realized that only six of my women were present. Morla was missing. Unable to restrain my impulses, I completed my pleasurable duties with the one scheduled for that evening, and in the common rooms, I asked about Morla. None had seen her since that morning.

On the veranda, or patio, I asked about her again. Again, none had seen her. For an instant I felt an alien emotion well up. *Could Lamoc or, the gods forbid, surly Khurko Tau-3, be mating with her?* My face clouded and my eyes searched for a weapon, anything that might enable me to reclaim my rights. Then the fit passed. My imagination was running free, I realized, influenced by the harsh events of the past weeks. It was inconceivable that any other male among us, any rational Mok-sa, could take the wife of another male, even the repellent Tau-3 who had sunk to the level of a primitive meat-eating carnivore. Catching sight of Lamoc across the patio, talking volubly with a drink in his hand and sitting on a bench, his beard wagging, I laughed at myself. My suspicions had to be nonsense.

Wandering about, I found myself behind the barracks where I often strolled after an evening's exertion, admiring the moons and inhaling the clean air of a brand-new planet. A single light shone through the only unblocked window on the back of the barracks, the window at the back of our common eating chamber. It cast its sheet of flame across the field of silvery stones where the rover and helicopter glinted. Trapezoids lit the faces of the two engineers again standing by the rover. Still obedient, still alert, while one of them heartily ate some delicacy from the kitchen.

Something darted from the darkness. It rushed to the distracted engineer. An upraised arm struck—he fell with a thud against the side of the rover.

The culprit stepped into the light.

In shock, I glimpsed tawny hair, golden skin, a perfect face, set in a new, strangely harsh expression. "Morla," I shouted.

She glanced at me—then the other engineer was upon her, attempting to wrestle her to the ground.

She fought back.

They rolled.

A knife flashed.

"Who? *Her?*" I wailed.

The engineer seized the hand that clutched the knife, and again they rolled. When they came to a stop, she staggered erect. How could I live with the result? The knife had penetrated one of her eyes, the blood streaming down her cheek. Like a madwoman, she snatched it out and plunged it in the chest of her opponent, who collapsed dead on the stones.

The other engineer shook his head as he regained consciousness. He too staggered erect. He grabbed a metal splint and brandished it, blocking the entrance to the rover.

Away she lurched.

"Murderer," the engineer shouted. "Running off will do you no good."

But she was not running off. In moments she arrived at the helicopter and she leaped behind the controls. In seconds she had it coughing.

I lurched to intercept.

The engineer was at my heels.

As we came near, Morla slammed the door to the craft shut, and with a jerk, lifted off.

The engineer and I dove under the propellors.

Moments later, the growling engine grew small in the night. My stunned eyes followed her course across the starlit sky. She was flying southwest.

Dragging myself back to the barracks, I could not help but morosely count the women left to my unit: only five. I spun and stared. Did a winged shadow just fly past me? Then it too was gone.

Chapter 9

The next day, no one wished to discuss the incident. Indeed, what could anyone say? The colony even calmed somewhat after more outrages by Khurko Tau-3. From somewhere he had secured another strip of flesh. An increasingly wild look shone from his eyes. When he saw me staring, he turned his back and hid his hand as if to conceal what he was eating.

After that I noticed another oddity. Several of the engineers began constructing a second barracks; not large and long like the first one, but smaller, and as I returned from performing my duty weeding the fields of Klopan, I paused to watch them work under the supervision of Yezd, this new barrack more sturdy with thick walls and a thick entrance door that could not be broken without extraordinary effort. Across the hundred yards distance I made out Khurko and Lamoc also watching, suppressed anger on their faces.

Could there have been a countercoup?

Yezd calmly supervised as if immune to the lynch mob.

A week later the second chamber was finished. I could not call it a full barracks as it was only large enough for a single unit of eight. When it was done, the entire Lambda unit moved in, vacating their quarters in the former building, their wall, which adjoined the Sigma unit in the first barracks, having been partly burned out.

We all need privacy at times, I explained to Little Milo. *There is nothing strange about that.*

What was strange was that once finished, and the door bolted like the gate of some medieval castle, the back windows were equipped with the usual glass that anyone could bust with a brick. Sensing something in the works, one evening when I had finished my husbandly duties with—dare I think it?—my *harem*, I lurked behind a convenient bush near midnight to see what could be seen.

Nothing happened, and I returned home in a bad mood, too late for any more conjugal coupling since my paramours had all gone to sleep, trying to adjust to the absurdly short Maalstrom days.

The next night was Asana's turn. But she was late and no one had seen her.

More perturbed, I decided to lurk again.

The white moon this time haunted the scene, throwing piebald loops as if sowing disease among mortal men. A small oil-lamp lit the inside of the one window on the back of the *castle* as I dubbed the new structure and I could see several of the Lambda unit females dallying within, and the male, whose name I had never learned, checking the door. Yes, that struck me as odd. Might they have heard in advance of another purity purge by the mob?

This night I was not disappointed. From the cover of the bushes, I saw the back window swing open, the women within exchanging cautionary glances. I could have sworn that something more was up than a raid by the local sheriffs.

Minutes passed.

An hour.

Still nothing, and the women and their male sat quietly within, one of the women holding something half-hidden in her lap.

Could it be? Inexplicably, I scanned the skies. A cloudbank hid the white moon and a wave of pitch-black swarmed over the landscape. Once more, my mind flew through a tangle of thoughts and suspicions, overwhelming me with fears and accusations. I had just made up my mind to emerge from my cubbyhole and walk boldly to that lit window, preparing to shout about hornets and infestations and midnight visits by nude malkops like the succubus of ancient myth.

A glint stopped me.

The glinting of an olive sliver of wing. The wind billowed. Something descended and landed before the open window, something large as a human, larger than I recalled concerning the native winged creatures. The wings folded and a dark splotch moved noiselessly into the window and blocked the light from the oil-lamp.

No shout of surprise or terror sounded from within.

What form of sorcery was this? I had heard of insects rendering their victim helpless, even taking over their minds and directing their actions to further the predator's life cycle, but how could I explain the collaboration of several rational Mok-sa women and their male in the presence of the beast?

I stood straight, the moon's white glare falling suddenly upon me.

That instant, three figures burst from another set of bushes and threw themselves upon the black thing that stood within the window-way and which blocked the interior light.

A trio of flashlights flicked on—bathed the thing in overlapping circles.

My heart stopped.

Olive-green scales flashed. Muscular solid arms. Two wings that were not bat-like, but translucent like the wings of insects. I searched for human eyes like that of the malkops I had thus far seen, and failed. In their place, a pair of wide-angled compound eyes like that of a dragonfly reflected the light from the torches a thousand-fold.

Two of the flashlights dropped to the ground and the men rushed upon the thing and cast a heavy net over it before it could retreat and spread its wings—Yezd and one of his engineers.

The net was cast.

The thing did not react.

Instead, it stepped forth calmly on its human-like legs into the diseased light of the moon where its nightmare features became all too visible. Taking the metal net in its hands, it effortlessly ripped it apart.

The wings flapped. It was gone.

Too late, Lamoc and Khurko and several more thugs emerged from the darkness, makeshift rifles in hand.

"Well, so much for your *nature-collecting*, Yezd," sneered Khurko. "Any more fine ideas about preserving the natural fauna?" Khurko kicked one of the flashlights, sending its ray of light spiraling into darkness before it flicked off. "Next time, we'll do it *my* way." Tau-3 snatched another surreptitious bite from his mysterious strip and shook his rifle like a confident hunter.

But all was not done.

I climbed confidently through the window. Lamoc smiled as if I had just joined their bloody posse. Inside, I halted to stare. Not knowing what I expected, or suspected, I snatched the cover from the lap of the Lambda female.

Three eggs. At least a week old.

Turning, I stumbled back into the clean night air. Behind me, the lynch mob brimmed with fury and crowded in. Shots exploded amid fire and gore, like the cracks of a frozen tree in winter.

Back to the bushes I rushed, lost what remained of my dinner. *When will I learn to leave well enough alone?*

I needed time. More time. I was not trained as a geneticist, but we were losing that skill as our best people disappeared...or were shot dead by the mob.

Rejoining the Mu unit, which, thank the rational god Teknos, was still intact and still interested in exploring our world, we ventured into the southern forest once more. They wanted to see the sinuous-necked amphibians and this time brought our only camera to collect detailed photos; I was more interested in smaller things and brought jars for collecting their life forms. It is the smaller things, in my view, that govern an ecology, proving their mastery over all by infinite reproduction.

On this occasion, we trudged deep into the forest, making sure to keep our directions straight. I glanced at the suns which had fully divagated signaling high summer, then we plunged into the semi-darkness of the vast forest.

No sooner did we cross the river where we had previously sighted the amphibians, than we found a narrowing where huge trunks had collapsed so that it was not too difficult to wade to the opposite shore.

There we halted at an unusual noise. Perhaps we should have finagled a rifle from the lynch mob. From somewhere not far distant, a savage roar had sounded followed by a squeal of some animal as if it had been viciously attacked. In less than an hour we stumbled upon one of the sinuous-necked amphibians. Its carcass lay in a clearing, its clawed feet upraised. From the shelter of the trees, we caught our breath as the new discovery filled us with caution.

A predator equipped with a single down-bent, bone-bare beak like that of a hawk, was tearing at the amphibian's throat with a great ripping off of chunks of flesh then swallowing them whole, its four thick-muscled legs sinking hook-like claws into its prey's body.

It was so intent on consuming as much of its prey as quickly as possible, that we were able to retreat softly back the way we had come. More of the predators could be heard roaring in the distance as if already alert to the kill. I swore never to venture anywhere again without a weapon.

Yet we persevered. Giving the predator a wide

circle, we reentered the thickets and only paused for the Mu male and his two female companions to review the photos of the predator they had managed to take. While they did this, I wandered a few steps farther, pausing only to brush away more fly-like insects after collecting a few. Thanks again to the gods that these at least did not sting and no slug-like leeches had attached themselves to our legs during our river crossing.

A dull flash drew my focus.

Pushing farther through a tangle of branches, I stopped. Just above me, ensconced in a fork of strong limbs was what appeared to be a flurry of translucent wings. Pushing aside my concerns about stinging insects, I worked my way close. Suspended in the fork was a ball of hornets, the same ones that we had termed *leroo-sa*, the very ones that had me so perturbed, the ones I suspected had something to do with what was happening to our colony.

Closer I edged. The insects seemed, peculiarly, to hang in the air; then I noticed more glinting and perceived that they were not suspended in air but were crawling about inside a translucent sphere of hexagons apparently made of glass, suspended in the maw of the two branches. Inside, the hornets crawled through what seemed to be tunnels, heading deeper in or crawling back toward the surface, where they came and took flight by the dozen, ignoring my presence.

Stepping closer, I attempted to peer through the corridors to see what was hidden in the center but could not see through due to their constant activity. Am I insane? Or just stupid? Their angry sting may be far more painful than their stealthy sting. I reached out and touched the sphere.

Immediately the hornets froze, no more movement to be seen. I still could not see to the center as the glass sphere lost its translucence and began to glow orange. In moments it changed to green then blue then violet.

Losing my nerve, I withdrew my finger. As quickly as the hive had changed, it turned back to blue then green then orange. Finally, it reverted to translucent and the hornets, which had begun a loud buzzing, resumed their business as if nothing had happened.

I tiptoed back to my companions. I did not dare to carry the hornet nest with me or any specimens, though I thought: *What would make a better subject of study given our situation?* But I was too cowardly to attempt it. At least, however, I had learned more about our...adversaries. I was now convinced that something fundamental had happened to us that involved these insects. And I had learned a bit more: some of the animals had displayed green, iridescent scales. And somehow, I felt that the glass of their nest would prove indestructible, that any attempt to shatter it would be futile.

Back at the barracks, I was not surprised to see everyone downcast, with Tau-3 and his new gendarmes policing the premises, propping doors open and taking some off their hinges, and boarding up windows, constantly scanning the skies for signs of angry malkops.

This was wrong. We should be doing the opposite. If my suspicions were accurate, the only cure, the only way we could restore the colony to its normal state would be to lock every door and hermetically seal the entire barracks and every room and not allow the women to exit into the open air. Who knew when our genetic code had been broken? The first month? The first week? The sting the *leroo* inflicted in stealth was barely noticeable, only a small welt that might have been missed.

No one had mentioned it.

Another development came as no surprise: Asana had not returned. She too was gone.

Now we were four. Can I even call that a harem? My Little One frowned at the notion, blasphemous as it was, but I could not help myself. My atavistic genes seemed to be surfacing.

The only warning, if it can be called that, was

Asana's last remark to Tlata, Tumsa, Bruna, and Mika: "Vensa thinks she has won. But I will bring her down." No one understood what she had meant and Vensa had been the first to vanish months ago. Now Asana was gone, apparently walking out of the camp in a southerly direction. Everyone had assumed she simply went for a stroll before returning to our soon-to-ripen fields of Klopan, which now needed less labor than before.

Staring across the outdoor wooden platform, I could see Yezd mixing with Khurko Tau-3 and his thugs without compunction. Dare I share with Yezd the results of my exploration? My cowardice took over again. Yezd had too much power. With his clashing yellow and blue orbs there was too much mystery about him, the reputation of Earth's Chaldeans, which was less than gilded, keeping me in my seat. He had stood by too calmly when my companions were slaughtered. Perhaps that is why Vedega Alpha-1 had left. *If* she had left. After all, a coup rarely allows the previous power-holders to continue breathing. They could not sit comfortably in their new seats if a countercoup were possible.

How about Rho-3 Lamoc? He too was coming and going, hobnobbing with the thugs alongside Khurko Tau-3. No, I could share nothing with him either. They were lost. All were lost. Unless I could find allies, someone, anyone. But there were none.

I watched the mob collect on the patio, polishing and cleaning their new rifles with hard looks on their faces.

That is when I made my decision.

Returning to my unit's quarters, I made sure that my remaining wives were inside, and cautiously, I locked our outside door. Through a crack in the window—the same that had allowed the hornet through the other day—I peered into the back area to verify that all was as I hoped.

Tlata was on especially good terms with Mika, if a little less so with Tumsa and Bruna, Tlata's psychologist training enabling her to smooth over everyone's feelings. In our conclave, I proposed my plan. No sooner did I do so, than the chaos outside began again. The lynch mob unleashed its latest foray, and as screams and shouts erupted, my paramours instantly agreed.

We had no time to plan. No time to gather anything but our most essential belongings.

We doused our oil lamp.

Together we ripped the boards off the back window of Morla's now empty room and crawled into darkness, no moon hurtling above to expose the landscape, for once.

From the far end of the barracks a flame burst forth. There was more resistance this time—gunshots rang out. Was the mob not waiting to line up their victims? Or had someone stolen one of the rifles and decided to shoot back?

We did not wait to find out.

Out of pitch-blackness we emerged to confront the two engineers, the flames playing on their eunuch faces as they stared worriedly at the commotion.

"It's a tangle, eh?" I casually uttered.

"What was that? Did Yezd send you?"

Tlata popped out of the shadows. "Yes. Yezd told us to make certain the rover is still here."

The first engineer shook his head. "Why wouldn't it be?"

The second engineer interjected, "We don't even know why we're guarding the thing. Except one of those crazed women killed our comrade." He glanced at the first engineer and I caught sight of a look that could only be slyness. The engineers seemed to edge closer to the rover's side door as if fearful someone might beat them to it. Could they themselves be planning to...

At Tlata's signal—my diffidence once more holding me back—Mika and Tumsa leaped on the first engineer and Bruna shoved him against his comrade. I threw myself against both their legs, sending them tumbling.

"No," one of the engineers shouted. "We were first."

As I stood, one guard grabbed my legs. The other grabbed the door handle and tried to drag himself inside—I glimpsed their boxes already loaded—the three women dragged him back out while I kicked my legs loose of the first guard's grip.

In another instant, we were inside. Shoving the two engineers back, we slammed the side door shut. I hurried to the controls while the women struggled to keep them from reopening the door.

The rover jerked.

Just as the rover seemed about to become airborne, the door yanked open. The darkness had returned but I sensed a body leap inside. The door again slammed shut.

Too late to investigate, we were off. A terrific yank of gravity flattened us to the floor and I sank impossibly deep into the cushioned driver's seat as the women were laid flat on the floor. I pulled the lever to direct us forward. Just to make sure no one on the ground interfered by firing a stray bullet, I jerked left, then right, until we were well out of range, then I flew back down to tree level.

In moments we were kilometers away.

Only then did I realize that the barrel of a rifle had contacted the back of my head.

"Don't turn, you *thief*," a low voice growled.

We were rushing through the empty night of Maalstrom. From somewhere a moon spanned the horizon free of clouds to throw a radiant blueness over the interior of the cabin. I saw only a glimpse out of the corner of my eye as four she-animals threw themselves at him who was holding the gun.

The rifle clattered to the floor.

Punching the autopilot, I leaped out of my seat and joined the fray. Five pairs of arms thrust our attacker into the sickly light—the face of Khurko Tau-3 grimaced and spat as the leader of the lynch mob squirmed to escape our grip.

All sanity seemed to leave him. "Eeagh! Malafak!" His eyes reflected the insanity of the night as Khurko spilled animal-flesh from his gibbering mouth.

Tlata was the first to speak. "What the hell? *How?*"

"Drop him from the rover," yelled Tumsa.

"How can we do that?" Mika fretted, struggling to keep her grip.

"Drop him? How can you think of such a thing?" Bruna shouted.

"Well, we can't fly all over Maalstrom with a crazy man among us," Tumsa shouted, ever the fatalist.

"Who says all over?" I yelled over the whine of the rover.

"Tie him up. I can't keep holding him," Mika shouted.

Tau-3 let loose a burst of energy and threw all of us off. I snatched the rifle and aimed it at his chest. "Calm down, my friend. Or you're done."

With that, he relaxed. Locating a fiber cord, Tlata and Tumsa secured his hands behind his back.

"Not so insane after all," I muttered.

In reply, he clamped his teeth on my arm, provoking a renewed struggle, finally to lapse again into wild ravings. Tying him to a handhold in the side of the rover, we at last managed to stand free, clinging to other handholds as the rover bucked over currents of air.

"So..." Tlata and Tumsa looked inquiringly at me, "what do we do?" Tumsa eyed the door.

"You can't," Mika yelled. "He is a Mok. He is one of us. A human. You can't just toss him out."

Tau-3 made no sign that he understood that his fate was being decided.

Continuing, Mika said, "Look at him. He isn't himself. How would you like it if some pathology took hold of you and someone tried to throw you out of a rover?"

"Pathology?" I frowned.

"Well, isn't that what it is?" Tlata replied. "It seems the entire colony has been seized with something, some kind of pathology."

I nodded. "You are right. Maybe he'll come to his senses once we settle down." I ignored my Little

One who looked at me like I was the one who was insane.

A figure slammed onto the windscreen—we jumped back, almost falling into the grips of the jabbering mess that was Tau-3. A blue-uniformed engineer had crawled up from beneath the cowl and now hugged the windscreen where he shouted, his eyes glued in terror to ours.

"Oh ye gods," someone blurted.

Another second and he was gone, swept into freefall.

I sighed, my own sanity suddenly restored. The women clutched each other like sisters and bawled while I returned to the driver's seat. After a time, they calmed.

Mika asked, "Where to?"

I adjusted the controls. "One guess. South by west."

Chapter 10

I don't know how long we flew. To me it seemed an eternity as the short Maalstrom hours hurried by, though I suspect I was suffering the same illusion as before when it felt like eons although it could only have been a few hours.

Dawn came and the dense forest that lay in a curve southwest of Klopus broke and gave way to grassland interspersed with more patches of trees, smaller and more stunted than the forest. After an hour or so, movement could be seen as if some ungulate herd were padding about but of color similar to the yellow grass, making details invisible from our height.

At length, a ribbon of blue broke the yellow, a river of some size that drained from the area around Klopus, which apparently was situated on a plateau, flowing south then directly west. A sharp bend in the river served to focus my mind.

"Mika, Bruna, Tumsa, Tlata...look below. A natural bend like that may make for an ideal defense."

They looked puzzled as they clung to their

handholds. "Defense? From what?"

"From *what?*" I let loose a headshake of disbelief. "How can you say *from what?*"

"Nothing has threatened us on this planet, except..."

"Nodding," I replied. "Yeah, *except...*" I threw a glance back in the direction we had come, "other Mok-sa."

"You can't mean what I think you mean?" expostulated Mika, she of the ever-present heart.

Tumsa threw in, "Haven't you been awake for the past few months?" Tumsa seemed to be evolving more to my way of thinking.

"I have." Mika glanced behind her as the rover swung in another air draft. "And now *he* is."

We looked at the rear of the rover where Khurko Tau-3 was still tied to his own handhold. He was awake but the wildness in his eyes burned brighter than ever.

"Is it agreed, then?"

"No," Mika shouted. "We are not throwing Tau-3 out of the rover."

Tau-3 made no sign he understood but merely breathed, wheezing slightly.

"I didn't mean that," I called over the noise of the motor. "I meant: Are we agreed to land the rover in the bend of that river below? Unit leader: Are we agreed?"

They peered through the screen.

Bruna nodded.

With a twist of the controls of the rover's ailerons and rudder, I sent the vehicle into a spiral and—determined not to sink its props into wet loam as had happened to Source—in another minute set the rover down as gently as I could on a large outcropping of rock.

Fortunately, the location had not only a defensible bend in the river, protecting us from three sides, and a clear top on the outcropping in case we had to escape by means of the rover, but also had thickets of broad local deciduous trees lining the river to provide us with shade. Even better, to the north, a broad open plain of yellow grass stretched to the horizon, giving us plenty of warning if anything approached from that direction.

After a careful scan of our surroundings through the screen, we hesitantly slid open the side door.

Just as hesitantly we stepped out, eyeing the trees for who-knows-what. Finally, we could risk relaxing. The air was cool and dry. The suns had completed their divagation, and in a few weeks would begin to merge, heralding the coming of what passed for winter here.

The clouds dissipated and after a short rest we

took an axe from the tools resident in the rover and proceeded to cut lumber to construct our own tiny barracks. We were all fit, all energetic as befit a crew that had been meticulously selected for strength, intelligence, and genetic flawlessness.

Covering the rover with a camouflage of greenery, we soon built a new barracks, tiny in comparison to Klopus, there being room for only the five of us and a kind of monkey cage for Tau-3 who still showed no sign of recovering his senses.

From behind stout wooden bars he glared at us and snapped his jaw like some beast. I draped a curtain over the bars to block his constant glare until we built a separate wing to house him, helping to preserve our sanity. Only my respect for Mika's tenderness kept me from contemplating tossing him over the cliff into the river to save us all the extra work.

When we discovered a water spring behind the rocky outcropping, we were overjoyed. We had found all we needed to set up our own little colony free from the insanity of Klopus, and presumably free from the menace of the malkops, though as an ecologist I still wished to unravel the puzzle of why they were so interested in us. And why I was so interested in them. For some reason I could not clear my mind of their ultra-feminine form, which stirred something within that even my paramours had not done.

Before many days were out, I found some time to rest in our new home after yet another labor-filled shift. Surrounded by my satisfied, if not entirely happy, unit-wives, I stared out the open door while my mind tried to untangle the knot.

I already knew why the malkops were interested in us Mok-sa; I just did not want to face the truth. Reluctantly and with alarm, I was forced to conclude that they were the product of a predatory insect-like species that we had overlooked when we had first landed and they had sought us out as an ideal naive prey in which they could implant their eggs just like the cuckold substitutes its eggs for the true offspring of its victims. The hornets expected us to raise their young — the white eggs — at the cost of our own.

But why fly off with our corpses? Why did they not speak though they plainly had mouths and emotions like us? And above all, what was the green-scaled thing I had seen in the Lambda quarters and which tore Yezd's metal net with ease? Was it too a malkop, but of some form not previously seen? Or were there multiple species preying on us?

I shook my head. There was no sense to it. There was no sense to any part of this alien world. And now we were only five, marooned, as it were, in a distant corner of the globe, hoping against hope that somehow we could at last manage to found our own little colony free of threat and fulfill our directives. Our duty was clear. The task more than ever unlikely.

The next day, with redoubled energy, I inspected every possible crevice and crack between my harem and the outside world, then made a fine-mesh net to cover the interior of the doorway to keep every possible insect blocked out at night. During the day, we could swat them away, but when we slept the bite of the hornet may not be felt. It must have been while we slept that we Mok-sa had been first infected.

A little Swiss Family Robinson we had become. I tried to look on the bright side. We were down to only five members, but we were surrounded by a vast new world of seemingly limitless resources such that we would not want for anything. Plentiful rain, fertile soil, a clean clear river by our side filled with new and strange but edible fish, as we soon discovered, fish that required merely wading into the flow to catch barehanded, apparently never before having been hunted by intelligent predators.

Yes, I confess, given our still difficult circumstances with no crop yet to be sown, we resorted to eating fish-flesh. No other flesh had presented itself to the bow and arrows we constructed, so at least we were not faced with the dilemma of emulating Khurko Tau-3. I was convinced that it was the chewing and eating of meat that had led to his insanity.

But there was more. Upon inspecting the strips of animal-flesh that Khurko had been surreptitiously consuming for weeks unchallenged by anyone, I discovered when we dragged him from the rover to his new cage that they were far from being the remains of lizards, as I had assumed. Rather they had been stripped from the flesh of our deceased Mok-sa. *Cannibalism.* That was how far his rational isle of logic had collapsed in the few short months since our arrival. In disgust, I threw the strips he still possessed into the river. I did not dare toss them onto open land for fear of signaling our presence to the malkops.

We decided to call our new little home *Ror,* after the constant roaring of the little waterfall caused by the flow of our spring cascading into the river. The river itself we dubbed the *Hedronmas,* after the rocky outcropping which is called a *hedron* in ancient Mok language.

One day Tumsa said to me, "We should fly the rover and see what lies around us."

I tilted my head. "Would that be wise? You know we cannot resupply its last energy stores. Can't we hike the vicinity just as well?"

"We haven't tested the rover in weeks. We should at least rise above the tree line and see if there is anything we should know about."

As the one chiefly concerned with the safety of our unit, even though I was not its leader, this struck home.

Mika joined us. "I want to go too. If I don't do something different, I will go as crazy as Tau-3."

"Me-3," added Bruna, not one to be left out.

"More-4," Tlata interjected.

Nodding, I went to the rover together with all the women and we piled inside.

"Up. Then down. My beloveds, we don't dare expend one iota more of energy than is essential. You never know when some surprise..."

They exchanged knowing looks. There was no need to explain the need to preserve a reliable way of quick escape.

I punched a series of buttons. The motor coughed awake. As the gravity neutralizer came alive we rose steadily into the air as easily as a balloon though not quite so soundlessly.

A hiccup echoed. The rover shook and lurched to one side. We had no opportunity to see anything but the tops of trees before it suddenly dropped.

"Handholds," I shouted. At the last moment before it contacted the rock, I managed to regain control. The hiccups stopped and the rover slowed.

I set it gently down.

With panicked breaths, we piled out as swiftly as we had piled in. For several minutes we stood and gradually calmed.

Kicking the side door, I spouted, "Something with the gears. That was not the neutralizer or the energy pack." Opening the front cowl like on an antique Spudz, I peered inside while the women stepped back.

Tumsa recovered first and shook her head. "If I have to stay in camp any longer, I'm gonna go berserk." Turning, she collected our only bow and our few arrows and filled a canteen with water.

Mika joined her. "I feel the same." The pair walked toward the edge of the outcropping.

Only Tlata stayed behind. "Don't come back..." she called after them.

I paused, horrified, and stared at her.

"Without finding something for us to eat," Tlata finished.

Tumsa replied, "I'll collect edibles in the wood later. Right now, Mika can use her pharmacology to examine the grasses on the open plain."

Carrying fiber-woven side-bags, Mika and Tumsa descended the rocky platform to the yellow grass below.

"Be back before dark," I called after them, putting on the airs of an outdated, old-world patriarch. I let loose an expression of authority, I hoped and my Little One laughed as the two ignored me and melted into the plain where patches of yellow altheas stretched to the horizon.

Back to the engine. I tried to put my concerns out of my mind. We were barely a colony even with the five of us, and I still had a duty to foster children as rapidly as possible. It was not all duty, of course. Youth and health also have their rights. But what could our tiny group accomplish with such a limited genetic pool? I focused on shaving a gear shaft until fatigue finally took me to our little hermetically sealed shack. Hoped it would work.

That afternoon a call brought me out as Tumsa and Mika emerged from the trees lining the riverbank and climbed the rocky platform.

Almost as soon as I greeted them, Mika halted. She looked back. "Oh, I forgot to collect some roots." She strode back down the slope into the open and walked some distance north and paused where I could see her small form bending and digging to place roots in her side-bag. Meanwhile, I sewed a tear in my white uniform, now faded and stained with gear oil.

Tlata looked at Tumsa. "How far did you go? Anything of interest?"

She shook her head. "We angled around to the Hedronmas. Lizards. Bugs. And more of those amphibians you saw up north. We watched them trot about in groups."

"I think I have a name for them."

A questioning look. "Another sacred act," Tumsa said.

"I christen them *revens*, or *reven-na*. As they are revenant on both land and water."

Tumsa stopped listening. Something had drawn her attention to the plain. On the horizon a black cloud had appeared.

Turning, I watched without alarm the black cloud spread as it rose high in the clear sky. I noticed a belt of red below and frowned. "Maybe..."

In the distance a soft drumming shook the ground. Tlata and Tumsa also looked, also puzzled.

At the limit of our vision, a thin line of yellow appeared, of a darker hue than the yellow of the endless grass and altheas. The tan line grew larger and undulated gradually, separating itself, the belt of red flaring occasionally behind it.

"Something comes."

For some reason I did not react. Tumsa and Tlata also stood mesmerized and silent as the line of darker tan moved in one direction, then another, then angled closer.

At last, Tumsa shouted. "Mika!"

She did not hear.

We all began to shout; leaped up, waved our

arms. "Come back, Mika!"

After what seemed an interminable length of time, Mika paused in her scavenging and saw us as she straightened.

"Come back now." We pointed at the horizon where the tan-colored belt gathered force as it neared, details becoming visible.

Uncomprehending, Mika stared.

The belt resolved into a herd of creatures unfamiliar to us. Racing on bird-like legs below a pair of grasping paws, their heads were striking: flat beaks surmounted by a pair of eyes, each temple sporting a thick bush of upright feathers, thin as needles. The heads spun about in rapid fashion, almost comically while the beaks repeatedly opened and closed in nervous response to real or imagined threats.

The mass neared Mika. Behind the herd, red flames sped through the grass, throwing up immense waves of smoke. The creatures were panicked, stampeding like similar herds on Earth after lightning triggered grass fires at the height of summer.

With similar danger?

"Get back now, Mika," I shouted, pointing.

Tlata made a move to rush to the plain to get Mika, but Tumsa held her fast. "It's suicide now."

The animals lurched left like a school of fish.

Just as suddenly flicked right. For an instant it seemed the herd would circumvent Mika. But the school lurched again. Before we realized what had happened, the herd swarmed over Mika's position.

She went down.

We hardly had time to suck a breath when the creatures moved away, still pumping their powerful bird legs, their beaks opening and closing, heads swiveling, the tufts of needle feathers shaking like clumps of ferns.

A memory flashed of smudges of darker yellow moving across lighter yellow grass, what we had glimpsed from the rover months earlier when Yezd was at the controls, and again when we had first arrived at Ror, but which we had not had time to investigate. Now we paid the price.

Hurrying down the rocky slope, we rushed out onto the plain.

Mika lay inert, torn and punctured by the birds' lethal splayed toes.

Gently, we lifted her and carried her back — lifeless is the word — to our shack. Tumsa, Tlata, and Bruna cleaned and covered her corpse through a mist of tears while I lingered by the entrance. I could not bring myself to assist in their funeral rites.

Nervously I scanned the sky for signs of...I could not bring myself to pronounce the name. Name the devil and he appears. I entered the shack and commenced to inspect every nook and cranny to make doubly sure no hornets would enter to take advantage of our sleeping hours. We four, of an initial colony of over two hundred carefully selected specimens, were perhaps all that remained.

Leaning on the front post, I stood suddenly straight.

Quick as we were in retrieving Mika, we had not been quick enough. Far above, sliding lazily in invisible air currents free of smoke, was a familiar form. A malkop. My heart sank. I had hoped that fleeing across hundreds of kilometers of emptiness would allow us to be free of them, but I had failed. Who was I kidding? Stepping away from the shack into open sunlight, I peered intently as I could into the nether and caught sight of several more, barely visible as they flew. Yes, I had been seeing them out of the corner of my eye since the day we arrived but I had not wanted to admit it.

Absent binoculars or telescope, all I could do was peer at their minuscule forms drifting among the clouds. They seemed to be traversing roughly east and west, or northeast from us. The single malkop that hovered closer soon abandoned us and also flew northeast...toward Klopus.

I could not stop my mind from racing. Except for cottony slips of cirrus high in the stratosphere and smoke from the fires, the sky was clear of clouds, but in my afflicted vision the sky seemed to roil and billow with the grey clouds of an impending storm. What lay to the west of us, downstream of Ror and our bend in the Hedronmas? The malkops could not fly forever. Might they also have a home?

I had to stay busy. Not only for my sanity, but to clutch the only solution I could think of, I stalked back to the shack and recruited the women, and after burying Mika in a deep grave behind the shack, we set about building two more rooms and a hall connecting all the rooms, and when this was done, I carefully sealed every crack that might let in the contagion. The women looked at me perplexed. I did not try to explain. There was something about their glances that made me nervous. Or was it *my* behavior that made *them* nervous? Might I be on the same path as Khurko, who remained as devoid of reason as ever, cackling from his cage even through the separating wall?

At last, all was finished, all constructed from lumber torn from several living trees along the Hedronmas bank, and sealant from sap collected by Tumsa, our botanist. We dared not venture onto the plains again but stuck to the rocky outcropping or shaded areas.

Thinking I might sleep for a century, at last I collapsed onto the only rough-hewn cot in our new communal dining area. The suns—already commencing to merge again after the high noon of summer had passed—threw their chiaroscuro loops across the landscape with the speed of a heartbeat as night plunged our little hamlet into darkness. Knowing our rooms were sealed and having no windows that could be left open, I allowed myself to fall into the abyss of unconsciousness as if administered a drug. Vast and with dreams so deep there could be no chance of later recalling them, I drifted lower and lower.

A sound clicked.

I failed to respond, my brain translating the sound into something that fit its absurd fantasies.

The click repeated.

My drifting reversed course, and before I understood, I was wide awake outstretched on the cot, darkness encompassing me except for a small light from the head of the hallway emanating quietly from our single oil lamp in Tumsa's room.

I cautiously sat up.

Stood.

Something had traversed the hallway.

With a start, I realized that for all my obsessing over seals and walls, I had forgotten to close the shack's front door when I had staggered inside.

Slowly I peeked out of the dining room and watched the door to the shack quiver to a slight breeze. With a rising sense of horror, I peered up the darkened hallway. The door to Tumsa's room was partly open, and a shadow passed over the lamp.

For a long moment I froze, unwilling to contemplate the enormity of what might be happening behind that door. Our sacred duties, our future, our labors...our very lives were at stake. Why did no sound come from inside Tumsa's room?

Silently, I stole up the shadowed hall; quietly I pressed the door wide.

In the light of the pale lamp all my fears coalesced in a moment, my fears concerning duty, effort, plans, hopes, trust in the motives and the lives of my treasured spouses for whom I had sacrificed so much and for whom I would have gladly thrown my very life away.

On the single makeshift bed that we had laboriously constructed for my beloved Tumsa, she lay supine, staring upward, the shifting light of her feeble oil lamp full upon her face. A look of indescribable contentment smoothed her features, an angled smile animating her as she lay nude and exposed, framed by the rough fiber sheets that beloved Mika had helped weave for her bedding. Her upward smile was directed toward something that I realized with a shock had filled my dreams with dread, something that leaned over her and even now clasped her nude form like a lover.

The thing that had torn Yezd's metal net with ease, that had hypnotized the Lambda unit including the male, the muscular malkop of hard green scales, ommitidious eyes, and translucent insect wings, was thrusting a proboscis from between its legs into her vagina. With each quiet thrust, she breathed heavily and smiled further.

I staggered—the fragile door slipped off its hinge with a crash—caught one glimpse of the face of Tlata who stood silently in one corner of Tumsa's room, an unprotesting witness.

Before I could snatch a breath, the creature rushed past, the wind almost flooring me. Outside, it took to the air with another current that slammed the outer door shut in its wake.

Tumsa broke into tears and covered herself with the fiber spread.

It was then that I glimpsed the unimaginable: flanking either side of Tumsa lay two perfectly round white eggs the size of baseballs.

Unable to look further, or unwilling to, I lurched out of her room. Locking the shack's outer door against the night and its demons, I fell back onto the communal cot and beat my head with my fists, anything to clear it and try to understand what was happening to her, to us, to me.

Chapter 11

S o now I know. Before, it had been only inference. Leading to a conclusion I had feared to accept. Now there was no avoiding the catastrophe: the green-scaled thing with the human-like legs and body but oh-so-insect-like head and wings must be a male version of the predatory species we had dubbed malkops. In the skies only those of the female gender were visible. At night the males came out to seek and inseminate Mok-sa women, to cuckold us with their alien offspring.

Standing outside the door in the clean air of the bright morning, I shook my head trying to force it all to make sense. Behind me, inside the shack, Tumsa still cried, still covered up. I could not bring myself to do what crazy Khurko and evil Lamoc had done. Though I possessed one of their makeshift rifles, I would not—could not—invade the shack and put an end to her. Not when so much was riding on the outcome of our venture.

Tlata entered to comfort her. Bruna, throwing a puzzled look at her co-wives, packed a satchel with food and set down the path to the tree-strewn bank of the river, headed west, departing with only a murmured, "Back soon."

I was too deep in my contagion to answer.

Midday, Tlata too took a satchel and descended the rocky path to the riverbank oppositely in the direction of the falls that flowed from Ror's spring. Lost in our thoughts, neither of us spoke.

When Tumsa emerged from her room soon after with dried tears and her own satchel packed with food—and her other *items*, which I guessed from the delicate way she carried the satchel—I said nothing but turned my head away. She attempted and failed to search my face with tear-marked eyes. Then she too left and set out directly across the open plain despite its dangers.

I gave her one glance as her tender form shrank across the vast empty plain headed north, then I returned to my cot, my Swiss Family Robinson seeming ever more like Robinson Crusoe...without a Friday.

I did not sleep for long, indeed did not sleep at all. Squirming like a squid in jelly I kept trying to force logic on what had happened to us, to all of us Mok-sa, as my ecologist superego fell back on its training, its education. A predatory species had obviously chosen us for its prey, and not just prey, but as repository for the sperm of the species' males. Yet, how to explain the human-like forms of what we had seen of the species, of both genders? Coincidence? I knew enough of the statistical unlikelihood of discovering humanoid forms on this planet to believe that their humanoid appearance could be mere coincidence. When we had landed, there had been no trace of the malkops. Now they seemed everywhere. Each time I glanced up, tell-tale dots crossed high above, at first singly, now in groups.

Wrestling with these facts I forced my ego to the only logical conclusion. Somehow our DNA had been broken, doubtless by the stings of the original hornets we had first encountered, the hideous *leroo*, whose sting was barely sensible. Many of us must have been stung, but only the women had suffered the consequences.

But why then would the malkop males bother to inseminate Mok-sa women? Weren't malkop females good enough for them? What on Maalstrom could drive a male to fertilize a member of a different species in preference to its own — assuming, of course, that we Mok-sa *are* different? What if we weren't? What if we were in fact not so different, but something closer?

I sat upright. Yet another disquieting thought had occurred. Back in Klopus, doubtless, many

Mok-sa women had been stung, which might explain why so many were giving birth to eggs, and why so many had voluntarily exiled themselves as Tumsa had just done, taking her eggs with her to keep them safe from the likes of Khurko and Lamoc, as if the birth of their eggs had triggered hyper-protectiveness.

But I myself had seen Bruna stung. Yet she alone had *not* become pregnant. She alone had *not* given birth to malkop eggs. And how to explain the strange acquiescence—even eagerness—of entire units of Mok-sa women to welcome the advances of the hideous male of the malkop species, though they had already given birth to its eggs? Or, if not to welcome, at least not to alert Mok-sa males outside of their unit as to what was up when a malkop male visited, as Tlata had just failed to alert me when the thing had visited us? Where have our contaminated women gone? And where do the malkops go when they rest from flight, as all winged things must?

Leaving the cot, I stepped out of the shack. Staring hard at the usual pinpoints of grey flitting between east and west, I thought I detected forms slowly descending at some point far to the west.

It was time to untangle the knot.

Leaving a note for Tlata, who I now was certain was preparing a safe place for her own eggs, I packed a satchel, bade Little Milo be calm, and climbed down the rocky slope of our little home to follow the path set by Bruna along the tree-lined riverbank westward.

Bruna must have the key.

Slinging the rifle over one shoulder by means of its attached fiber cord, I attempted to trace Bruna's path but soon failed. Opting to walk parallel to the river where the trees petered out into plain, I made progress, and by the end of the short Maalstrom day I found a fork in a tree in which to sleep. Who knew if the sharp-beaked carnivore I had seen tearing apart the reven wandered here also? After a fruitless hour of painful positioning, I gave up and descended to sleep on the ground, predators or no predators.

Waking with sunrise, I spotted another *leroo* hornet and angrily smashed it flat. Then started out again.

More rocky outcropping rose to the north, forcing me to wend my way through a narrow gorge until suddenly the plains opened up again. For a time, the trees vanished and I was able to walk along the bank of the Hedronmas. The river had widened and I could see open plains on the opposite bank stretching to the far southern horizon. In the most distant south, a range of mountains glimmered. What a vast, rich, fertile rock this Maalstrom was, spinning its speedy way through space, with its five gorgeous moons, three of which even now graced the sky with their pale round plates.

A small herd of the bipedal birds strolled to the north. I could only hope that Tumsa had not met the same fate as Mika and would arrive safely wherever she hoped to go, even if she herself would only give birth to more malkops. *I know, Little One. More sacrilege. But we Mok-sa are human after all and don't humans wish the best for other humans? But malkops are not human*, I reminded myself. *Or are they?* Swiftly, I halted that line of thought.

In truth, I knew nothing. Yet.

A week passed and the scrub along the riverbank appeared, spread, disappeared, then mushroomed into green forest again. And still I followed the river, confident that intelligent Bruna would do the same in order to avoid the dangers of the open plain and its wild habitants.

I had entered a darker patch of trees where the gradually merging suns, indicative of the coming of autumn, barely penetrated with random rays when a glimmer attracted my eye. At first inclined to dismiss it, I passed by. But then halted. Something shiny? Tree sap does not occur in the middle of an open glade. Returning, I approached to investigate.

Brushing aside leaves, I stared.

A satchel lay on the ground. I picked it up and peered inside. An assortment of edible roots, some locally procured vegetables, and a tin foil packet with the insignia 'Psi' printed on it.

Bruna's satchel.

Why would she discard her only ready source of food? I searched the glade, peered into the bush surrounding the glade, gazed upward into the trees. Nothing. There was no sign of Bruna. But something must have happened to her as she would not dare to leave her stores. Shouldering her satchel next to mine, I pushed hurriedly into the forest beyond, no trace of any path available to me.

A half-day, a day, another night huddled beneath a towering tree while hoping no predator, known or unknown, would pick up my scent. Then I pushed on, again deciding to favor the more open terrain where the riverine brush melted into open plain. Almost unconsciously, I eyed the skies for the telltale signs of malkop presence and found myself yearning for another glimpse of their beautiful forms while harshly suppressing the memory of the green-scaled males with their ommitidious eyes. My progress increased.

Once I paused in the open when a—how should I say—*flock* of half a dozen malkops swarmed overhead, lower than before, and flew westward where I could swear they seemed to descend at some point. The reaction that this glimpse aroused in me is difficult to describe. They are not us—they *cannot* be human—so why do I find myself aroused at the very sight of them?

Still, after that, I decided to avoid the open and returned to traipsing through the forest. If I were to approach their terrestrial habitation, I wanted it to be on my terms with no alert coming from these denizens of the sky.

Another leaf-bowered aisle in semi-darkness. Another semi-rayed glade or two. The suns, slowly merging and hearkening cooler weather, and I was forced to halt as the foliage became too dense to proceed.

Securing my two satchels on one shoulder, and my rifle over the other, I bent the wild growths to either side and thrust my way through and emerged into another open glade where the suns' full glare bore down.

My eyes met the oddest sight that I could ever have expected: a pair of eyes much like my own stared back.

Instantly I froze.

Cautiously, a figure emerged from the brush, blocking my course. Step by step it came closer until it stood full in the suns, not two meters distant.

A man—or more precisely, a boy—at any rate, distinctly human, male, and young, if its small size was evidence of such. The face was clear, no trace of beard, a brown loincloth hiding its lower half, its half-muscled torso and shoulders crisscrossed by a quiver of arrows and a taut bow. As if to emphasize, the boy raised the bow at me with arrow nocked. There was no smile to indicate friendliness. Instead, the boy pointed at my rifle and motioned for me to drop it.

I was too preoccupied by the wildness of the boy's feathered hair, which reminded me, in its manifold shape, of pictures of ancient Gauls, and he bore a series of intricate blue and black tattoos like ancient Britons or Picts.

Seeing that I did not obey, he whistled. At once, a half-dozen more figures emerged from the forest, equipped with arrows and flint-tipped spears, each boy similar in appearance, of perhaps twelve or thirteen years of age by Earth standards. But who knew how many years by the short span of Maalstrom years?

It seemed I had stumbled onto the only truly intelligent life on the planet. That they seemed as human as I made me question this, question everything. Humanoid malkops were one thing; actual humans quite another.

"Let it go," the first boy spoke. Too surprised at hearing the first voice from a non-Mok creature of intelligence in my entire life, and in my own language, I instinctively dropped the rifle. I stared dumbly, my mouth open.

A second boy stepped forward. He retrieved my rifle. For a moment he examined it, his face perplexed. Apparently thinking it a form of club, he held it by the barrel and swung it. Then he gave up trying to understand it and hung it upside down across his shoulder opposite his quiver.

Looking back at the first boy, apparently their leader, I exclaimed, "Why...*you can speak*. You can speak our language, the language of Mok-sa."

The first boy shrugged. "There is only one speech. How could the children of Vensor prevent chaos if Vensor's children could not understand each other? A crazy idea." He looked me over with contempt. "From a crazy foreigner."

"Foreigner?" I asked in surprise.

"Huh. We have known about you since you arrived. As long as you kept away. But now..."

It seemed everything this day would be surprising. But now... *what*?

"Enough of foreigners. We know what to do with such as you. All of you. We have been instructed."

Among his tattoos I noticed a motif of a familiar animal and pointed at it. "So you like reven-na? So do we Mok-sa."

The boy silently mouthed to himself *reven-na*

as if memorizing the term, then glanced down at his tattooed chest. "They are sacred to my clan. Sacred to Vensor." He glanced up at the double suns, then at his companions. "So are many creatures."

Peering, I perceived several different motifs among the tattoos, apparently clan insignia. Some bore the stripped bone beaks of the jungle predators I had seen consume the luckless reven back at Klopus; others were of animals I had not yet seen.

"Enough talk, foreigner. The Temple will open soon. We must hurry or we may miss the calling for sons." The entire crew of tattooed, headdress-feathered, half-nude, barefooted but very well-armed and confident boys surrounded me, and a few well-aimed pricks from their flint spears forced me forward. At least it was the direction I wished to go.

Only then did I put it together. "All of you" could have meant only one thing: they had found Bruna. However, I had no opportunity to pursue conversation as my little escort pushed me headlong into the brush where, whenever I fell behind, more spear pricks urged me to keep up. I wondered if going barefoot was an advantage but dared not remove my shoes for fear I may never see them again.

Chapter 12

A day passed. I grew too exhausted to talk. More feathered boys joined us to boost their numbers to a solid score, some armed with long wooden pikes, others with scored metal blades, which made me wonder if we were heading for some industrial fount that had been hidden from the rover's surveys.

No smokestack appeared, however. And no sounds to indicate industrial-type production, only the soughing of the soft wind as it swept the eternally whipping clouds from my confused mind as much as from the confused sky.

Finally, we paused to rest. The silence was entrancing as I sat waiting for my tired legs to recover. To my surprise, I realized I did not miss the busy-ness of Earth at all, or the constant beeping and energy transfers of our ship Source, or the clattering about at Klopus as our hyper-scientistic Psis, Rhos, and Pis rushed about with the aid of their eunuch engineers, never having a moment's rest, their minds never calming, never relaxing, not once enjoying a Nature devoid of noisy modernity. I found I missed none of my former life.

At times I found I even envied these little wild savages in their feathers and primitive clan insignia like Cro-Magnons. Still, I could not forget why I had come, why I had cooperated: I needed to know what had happened to Bruna. Not just whether she still lived, but why she seemingly, alone of all our Mok-sa women, had not become pregnant and given birth to malkop eggs.

I could not forget Tlata either. That she was somewhere close to Ror I felt certain. Just as I was certain that she had become like Tumsa. Just as all our women would become, perhaps had already become back in Klopus, assuming the lynch mob had not insanely murdered every remaining female.

The *terminus ad quem* of every civilization. Even my Little One didn't miss it but he was also too tired for his usual smirky remarks. With a signal from our leader, the reven-initiated boy, I was jerked up and pricked into a resumption of our expedition, bringing my forlorn reverie to a close.

Our hasty impetus resumed and for another short Maalstrom day and a half (twenty-one Earth hours, my scientistic mind calculated) we pushed along the riverbank to the west, ever west, though we did finally avoid the denser thickets lining the shore and favored the lighter brush as it petered out into open plain. Apparently, there was less danger from stampedes by the land birds with fires no longer on the plains.

Pointing across the plain, I imitated the bipedal birds.

"Rum-na," the reven-clan chief muttered without emotion before hurrying me forward again. Another sacred name.

Before us loomed a rocky outcropping much like the one at Ror, which led me to conclude that wherever we were going we had arrived. To the north, perhaps a kilometer off, I saw another tree-tangled thicket lining what I concluded was another river, the outcropping situated in the Y of their union.

A curved row of stakes appeared, angled outward, ready to impale any unfriendly visitor. Each sharpened and fire-cured, with only a single narrow passage snaking a path through. By the entrance, another half-dozen clan-tattooed boys of similar wild appearance pointed pikes and arrows at us until determining we were safe to allow in. Leaning over on my knees to catch my breath, I heard my Little One offer an intelligent suggestion for once: their alertness suggested more than defense against mere animals.

Then I was pushed through the angled pathway and into the intrados of the row of stakes.

I was taken aback by the sudden appearance of boys of younger ages, from children to near toddlers as they ran about in play and mock combat amid a sprawling complex of thatched huts. A phalanx of older boys were building more huts and tending a small field of yet-to-develop plants, while yet more tended to the needs of the youngest. Little Milo at once perceived that every boy we saw had a specific clan tattoo, even the smallest.

Tired of surprises, I dumbly noted in my fatigue—did these active little children never tire?—that a second row of stakes edged around an indentation in the rocky outcropping, which ascended at perhaps twenty degrees to the northwest. The broad Hedronmas curled to my left where it joined the second river emerging from behind the outcropping.

My escort was not done. I was again pushed forward up the slope toward the cleft. From it flowed a substantial creek. Clearly a spring lurked somewhere under the rock. *Quite a nice location for a settlement*, I reflected, *much better than Klopus. If only these little savages had not already staked their claim.*

More little warriors guarded a barred gate that led through the second line of stakes. Here we halted as the two groups spoke quietly, *tête-à-tête*.

My escort, now reduced to a mere four 'mature' boys of perhaps twelve Earth years, pulled me back and motioned that I sit, for which I was more than grateful and I at once stretched out on powdery soil, feeling like a relic in a wild new world.

The boys also sat, not only my reduced escort, but as I watched, every boy in sight squatted, waiting calmly, for what I could not guess.

In a few moments, however, a clanging erupted from within the stony cleft to reverberate along its sides until it dominated the entire settlement. All activity ceased and the boys broke out in quiet song. All I gathered was something about a god named Vensor, and ending with a shout, they leaped and pointed their weapons at the double sun. I remembered my captors' urgency in returning in time for something they had termed the Calling For Sons and felt this must be it.

They fell quiet again.

Then came the most mysterious development heretofore of my long eventful life.

From within the second line of stakes came a sudden wailing of tiny throats. The gate to the second line of stakes opened and the older boys rushed forward, for once ignoring me. I stood and cautiously thrust my head through the gate and laid my eyes on a yard strewn with a dozen to all appearances human babies, each struggling its little limbs, each crying with all its might.

"Praise Vensor," the mature boys shouted

before rushing into the yard and retrieving all the infants which they took out of the gate and soon separated into groups: the property of separate warrior clans, I presumed. In confirmation, I noticed that the infants immediately received the first of what I was certain would be extensive tattoos as they grew older, denoting a lifetime of animistic clan loyalty.

I was more than perplexed. Every law of nature that I knew of divided mammalian species into equal numbers of male and female. If a hundred boys were visible here, somewhere there must be a hundred girls of similar age, and up to fifty adult couples who produced them.

The gate remained open. My escorts again surrounded me and led me through it into the now empty yard. Here was finally something that made sense. The creek ran under the line of stakes from out of the cleft.

A dozen older boys entered the cleft, bearing an assortment of food items, impressive given their young age, including trophies of the hunt with dismembered parts of the bird-like bipeds they had called *rum-na*, and slabs of meat from some larger animal I had not seen, along with baskets of wild fruits and vegetables.

With these presents at our head, my captors snaked inside with me in tow. Just before we entered, I could have sworn I glimpsed a flutter of wings above the outcropping as of something descending, and my confidence rose that I was at last on the right track.

Inside, I noticed that there was no need for torches, since far ahead light was filtering in. After a short stretch of perhaps twenty meters, the rocky sides of the tunnel opened suddenly onto a wide interior cavern where I received another shock. I was not sure how much more my Little One could stand before he bawled or exploded in frustration.

Blocking us was yet another wood fence, this time a high palisade with an open gate, and an open space on the hither side. Here the boys deposited their food items with care on the bare ground amid the dirty stone before stepping back to watch. Only then did I notice in the feeble light that seemed to emanate from farther up the cavern a primitively carved totem. More than anything else it reminded me of those impossibly ancient statues dug up by our ancient ancestors, statues of solar deities with aureoles, a golden fan about the head of each in imitation of sunrays. This totem was two meters tall, consisting of mostly a single round body of plaited yellow straw, its clumsily shaped arms and legs tiny in comparison. And more: beside it sat upright the severed head of one of the older boys, apparently executed by his fellows for some sacrilege.

The boys focused their eyes on this totem, and again I heard the shout: "Praise Vensor!"

Then the gate in the palisade opened. And my Little One bawled.

Out of the gate hurried over a dozen girls of similar age, including young ones who obviously could not lift or carry more than a pittance, yet who helped the older females with alacrity. Minutely I inspected them as they swarmed over the gifts and carried or dragged them inside the gate; I spied more girls standing on platforms staring down at us over the palisade.

They wore the by-now familiar brown cloths, though theirs seemed better sewn and cleaner than the wild savage boys of the outer settlement, and their cloths encompassed their entire body leaving only head and hands free. Apparently, unlike the boys, the girls had a degree of modesty.

The gift-giving done and their gifts accepted, most of the boys turned and filed back out of the tunnel, leaving only my original captors by my side. For a moment I stood nonplussed. Do I go farther? Or was I to be turned away without having any of my questions answered?

The palisade gate began to close.

Momently I thought I spied a familiar face staring down at me from the high palisade—then it was gone. In the dim light I could not be sure. *Could it be?*

Just before the gate shut, one of the older girls appeared in the gap, halting it. She caught the eye of my captors and pointed to the tunnel. My escort promptly exited and abandoned me. Well, I concluded...it seems I myself am one of the gifts, perhaps why I was still breathing. A gift to whom? And for what?

The gate opened wider, and a half-dozen girls—a few of whom I suspected were starting to show signs of maturity, sooner than the boys—exited. Brandishing their own smaller version of flinty spears, they surrounded me. I don't know if I was relieved to have my little adventure continue, or shaken at what seemed my uncertain fate, but they inspected me closely before ushering me through the gate to the nether side of the palisade. I noticed one of them clutching my rifle, again like a club, reassuring me that whatever awaited, the chance of a firing squad was remote.

Thus, I encountered the first chamber of the Sacred Precinct of the City of Ven.

Verging the lip of a low rocky spine, I opened my eyes to a flood of luminous minerals set in the walls and saw plainly what I had begun to guess but had not confirmed. Strewn over a carefully cleaned floor of undulating stone lay a double row of what I could only describe as large purplish lozenges.

My female escort ushered me past the lozenges, which were carefully tended by several girls who appeared even younger than the ones armed with the flint-tipped spears. I found myself in a second chamber that housed more eggs. These were smaller than the magenta lozenges and oval-shaped. More girls of tender age were tending to these, feeding them what looked like a milky substance, and here the eggs responded with squirming and a faint mewing, audible over the rushing stream. Yes, exactly what I had witnessed in Klopus.

The interior of this part of the cavern was still in semi-darkness, but my mind reeled with tangled emotions, hope mingled with despair. What had we innocent Mok-sa colonists stumbled upon? On what sort of planet were we marooned?

I was permitted no chance to think, to recover. On we plunged. My stunned gaze fell upon at least a score of small white spherical eggs tended by yet more underage girls, all dressed, as were my escorts, in gowns of sewed cloth—or was it the skins of slaughtered animals?—that covered their bodies leaving only their legs and arms exposed. These eggs too seemed to squirm slightly as their nurses fed them tiny quantities of the same milky substance. Somehow, I felt it was not powdered milk.

Without warning, a breeze blew a charnel scent upon me and I almost wretched. My escort of girls seemed not to notice and only hurried me forward once more. Overhead the luminous chemicals in the stony outcropping glowed pink and revealed the latest roiling revelation: stretching across the cavern at its widest part was a series of hexagons of silvery roughly formed bricks, each hexagon approximately four meters in width and all joined into a single structure that marched across the expanse of the cavern, the rushing stream circling to one side as it sought the nearby river.

Each hexagon housed a single centrally located tree, though how any tree could survive without sunlight I could not imagine. Upon closer sight, I saw that they were not trees but something *like* trees, their trunks glittering pink like the ceiling.

Breaking from my captors, I leaped into the nearest low-walled hexagon and touched one. The bole's surface gave way like putty and I concluded they were a variety of fungus. I recoiled and rejoined my captors who stood exchanging glances as if uncertain how to handle my transgression.

Only then did it hit me. Inside the hexagon I had tread upon bodies of the dead. Shaking, I peered back across the nearest low-walled enclosure of bricks and looked down upon a field of corpses...corpses that were clearly human. It was difficult to make out details in the poor light, but there was no mistaking the outlines of human torsos, human legs, human faces. Many wore the white uniforms of my Mok-sa...*so many*. The situation in Klopus must be worse than I feared. Half our colony must now lie beneath these death trees in this little city of savages.

At least one of my questions had thus been answered. I had at last found the terminus of the malkops' theft of our dead. Even as I stared, a flapping of wings disturbed the charnel air and a pair of malkops flew in from the far end of the cavern with their grisly burdens. Hovering over the nearest hexagon, the malkops dropped their two white-clothed Mok-sa before flying up. One corpse rolled before stopping at my feet to gaze at me with empty eyes. I caught my breath: it had a black beard—it was Lamoc Rho-3, with a gaping hole in his chest as from a rifle shot.

So there is some justice in the universe after all, my friend.

The malkops hovered near the tops of the fungus trees where they devoured strange fruit of the fungus with relish. Two alighted on the ground where they seemed intent on shaping a pair of new bricks with spew from their mouths, which they placed on one of the low wall of bricks surrounding the fungus trees. Then all flew higher.

In the center of the catacomb stood a cylindrical tower, or altar, not high, but tall enough to ensure no interruption as to what transpired at the top. Distracted as I had been by the smell and the revelation of what had happened to the bodies of my comrades, I only now perceived in the luminescent glittering of the cavern a half-dozen of the older girls carrying several of the purplish lozenges. Approaching the tower, the older girls climbed up one side, which was apparently equipped with handholds, and with some effort, deposited the lozenges on the top platform before climbing back down.

When they had stepped away, the next miracle occurred. The malkops, who until now had hovered as if in wait, alighted on the tower. I knew what would result when the lozenges tore, which began even as I watched. I had seen it with my own eyes back in Klopus when the infant malkop emerged only to be murdered by Khurko.

A wave of sympathy washed over me. What had these malkops ever done to us Mok-sa except to recycle our dead without offering us any harm? Hadn't we Mok-sa done exactly the same with our custom of letting our own dead decompose in our grain fields? Yet *we* called *them* vultures. Only the males inseminating Mok-sa women whom they had somehow hypnotized into passivity were to blame for what had happened to us. So far, I had seen no male malkops anywhere, except at night when the males had committed their heinous deeds in Klopus and Ror.

I pointed to the female malkops and glanced back at my captors, who briefly paused. "Selks," the oldest girl said, a look of surprise on her face as if everyone knew that.

So that was their sacred term for the malkops.

I had no time to contemplate. As the first lozenge broke and the little one emerged to test its wings under the happy gaze of its winged comrades, my escorts hurried me forward, out of the charnel cavern, paralleling the hurrying water until we arrived at a high stony lip at the base of which stood a half-dozen older girls. Counting, I concluded however that their number amounted to nowhere near the quantity of males inhabiting the outer settlement. The boys seemed to outnumber the girls ten-to-one. As an ecologist, I had thought that come what may, Nature will out. Not here on Maalstrom?

Then it struck me. I had already seen how half the eggs matured into males and were placed outside for the wild boys to retrieve and to raise as hunters and warriors. I had seen how a few of the eggs had matured into girls who tended the eggs in the cavern. Now I had seen how a larger number became magenta lozenges, which the girls hoisted upon the platform and which become female selks.

They were therefore all the same. All were siblings, including the malkops.

Over the lip of the small ridge thrust a face—a flush of recognition, then I was motioned to bend low and avert my gaze and the girls pulled me down by my arms, still giving me no time to think.

I could no longer contain myself. "Bruna. My Bruna."

Straightening, I sought to see her again, but the face I had thought I recognized melted into another with violet eyes. For several moments it seemed alien, that of a stranger. Then it burst upon me.

"Vensa," I yelled, the girls at my side no longer able to restrain me.

The face rose higher, now joined by Bruna's face, and Vensa motioned to the girls to bring me to a gap in the stony ridge. I rushed through and stepped into the full light of the double suns. Its glare through a wide opening in the cavern above made me cover my forehead with a palm.

Before me gurgled and eddied the source of the spring as it bubbled from beneath a stony wall that formed the end of the cavern before settling into a pool and gushed out one side to form the stream that flowed the length of the cave until it emerged in the settlement to flow at last to the river.

With malkops whirring overhead, retrieving the dead and helping young ones just learning to fly, I gazed upon the sight that unhinged my sanity...and calmed the shuddering Little One at the same time.

My mate, Vensa Psi-6, our best biologist from my very unit, was nude as during our most intimate bedroom encounters. She slid her bulk back into the pool where the gravity was less and from where her attendants—all girls mid-range in age between eight to ten Earth years as near as I could tell and all modestly clothed—hurried to bring her samples of the food items that the boys had provided to the inner sanctum with such profusion, items secured from energetic hunting and scavenging.

"Yes, Goddess," I overheard the little ones murmur as Vensa pointed a plump finger to a ripe fruit, and again to a strip of cooked rum-na flesh, bird feathers still clinging. She consumed them with the haste of one starving.

No longer capable of outrage at the eating of meat, I focused instead on the shallow pool where a score of white eggs drifted, gradually floating to the water's surface where the girls waded about and collected them with tender care, caressing each as if made of gold. The younger girls, too small to enter the pool, accepted each in a protective embrace and carried the eggs to the waiting arms of older girls. And thusly, until they must arrive at the egg-drying and egg-nourishing chambers past the cemetery of fungus trees.

My eyes hastened to Bruna, who stood alongside the pool. Her face glowed with love as she trembled, her arms reaching out of their own to me. She was ever close. But now?

"Bruna. I followed you. Found your satchel. The boys relieved me of it along with my own. I feared the worst." I glanced around. "Have they treated you..."

Bruna smiled and her arms fell back down. "Milo. I have no reason to complain. The boys escorted me here, they said they had strict orders."

"Orders for what? They could not have known you or known me."

"*My* orders, Milo." Vensa's plump hands clung to a lip of rock on one side of the pool as she steadied herself in the swirling water. Her face melted into the same gorgeous violet-eyed paramour whom I had also loved in my prior life — a life that had become so primordial that I could scarce remember details. Only the lovely faces and the lovely eyes of those whom I had so recently met before our fantastic voyage to this planet and who, within such a short time, had possessed my soul.

"You are beautiful as ever, my love," Vensa purled, her still luscious lips curled in a convincing smile as she spoke. "How I wish..." She glanced down at the water, watched the young girls dutifully skim white spheres from the surface. "We knew each other so briefly, but I loved you so much. You must know that, Milo. I wanted to spend the rest of my life with you." Vensa's violet eyes grew sad. "But you would not leave the others. You would not make me number one, your one, your only." Did a tear appear? "I cannot live that way. In a harem."

I nodded. "You were always the jealous one, Vensa. And I could not live with that. Not when we had a duty to colonize this planet, to populate it as fast as possible. Couldn't you understand that I had a duty to mate with the others in our unit?"

Again she smiled. "Yet, who is succeeding?" A chuckle erupted from her.

I frowned. "You mean to say—"

"You still refuse to see what is before your very eyes?"

I huffed. "Nothing has happened, Vensa, except that a species of predatory wasp of this planet has used us for its prey. Has used us Mok-sa as receptacles to implant its seed, or its eggs, which then grow into female malkops and predatory males. This planet has destroyed us, all of us, has killed our colony, our colony which was the last hope of humanity."

Vensa laughed, her torso splashing the water. "You still cannot face it, Milo. How can you, a planetary ecologist, not see what to me, only a biologist, is so clear? We once spoke of ironies. This is irony of ironies."

Bruna spoke up. "I think he understands now, Vensa."

Nodding, Vensa spread her hands open to left and right. "All this, Milo. All that you see. These are *all* my children, even the selks, whom you call malkops, or *vultures*."

"Please tell him the rest, Vensa. What he does not know."

"If he can take it, Bruna. Look. His face is strained and stiff. But *We* are ever-gentle, ever-forgiving." Vensa pulled herself closer, almost climbing out of the spring onto the rocky floor and exposing full her swollen human breasts. "These children, Milo...most of them are *yours*."

My eyes narrowed in confusion.

"Yours, Milo. You are the father of at least half of them." Vensa winked at Bruna then smiled. "Well, I did have a thing for the Delta male, Karol, if I recall his name right." She chuckled again. "And of course the males from Zeta, Kappa, and Chi, who also could not keep their hands off me, whatever their names were."

I straightened as if struck.

She continued. "The moment I realized I was pregnant, I knew what I had to do. My instincts told me what was necessary. Even before the first egg arrived, I knew I had to mate with all the men that I could, and when the first egg came, I packed my things and left Klopus to embrace my instincts, my destiny. They led me to this spring seeping out of this cave which I saw was a natural refuge. I entered and I dug this spring with my own hands, freeing the flow which was mostly blocked. I lined this pool with my own hands. By then my eggs were coming. First by ones and twos, then a half-dozen at a time. The flow of my eggs grows greater with each day, Milo. With each bright dawn, the number of my sons who protect my Sacred Spring from intruders and the number of my daughters who tend to my needs inside its walls, and the number of my daughter selks who have their own duties to perform in the air...the number of them will keep growing until my children swarm the surface of this planet with their numbers. *That* is my destiny. *That* is our success."

The light of understanding was growing inside me.

"You see, Milo?" Vensa added, "Our colony

did not fail. It succeeded. It succeeded beyond all expectations."

"But Vensa. How could you or any other Mok woman voluntarily submit to that *thing?* That insect-like male malkop that hypnotized and then fertilized you?" I spoke loud, outraged.

She shook her head as if confused. "I mated only with humans, Milo. I accepted every male I could until I had collected all the sperm I needed to make me divine. And it was me doing the hypnotizing, not the Mok-sa males whom I seduced."

Deep inside me, I stared at Little Milo, thinking: *Could she be right? Could much of what I believed I had seen been only hallucinations? After all, the insect visitations had occurred only at night when I was exhausted and half-asleep.*

Vensa resumed, "I now have within me the means of immortality. Long after you die, long after all the children you see in my city grow old and die, I, their Queen, will still be young, still giving birth to eggs, still be what I am now, a Goddess, worshipped by all." A look of triumph shone on Vensa's gorgeous face. I could almost worship that face myself.

"But Bruna?" I threw a longing look at my other erstwhile favorite.

Vensa looked down and shook her head. "She

must remain here. I need her expertise to train my daughters. To keep them from running off, especially as the girls grow into women and women's desires take hold." Vensa's voice turned harsh. "My daughters become ungrateful and abandon me. Several have already left. Including my oldest and first, my daughter Nesta, who fled the moment the signs of adulthood appeared. After she left, I commanded the boys to build a strong palisade, not just to protect me from outside dangers, but to keep my daughters from fleeing to found their own cities and compete with me. And to prevent my daughters from consorting with the fast-growing boys as my daughters grow equally quickly into women. My daughters may not mate. Only I, their Goddess, can give birth. They shall remain my priestesses, unwed virgins, for their entire lives. Indeed, I have instructed my warriors to escort back to me any female they encounter anywhere in the outer world...and to prevent my daughters from ever stepping beyond the palisade alone. My daughters have one job only: to spend their lives taking care of their Goddess. They can have no other."

"And...what if Bruna is pregnant?" I directed a stronger look of outrage at Vensa. "Would that not threaten your *empire*?"

"She is not." Vensa shrugged. "And as long as

she lives she shall not become pregnant. So I have no issue with my dear Bruna...so long as she is loyal and performs her required tasks. Else I may have to think of some appropriate punishment."

I recalled the severed head I had seen outside the palisade's gate. That must have been the result of one of Vensa's 'appropriate punishments'. What was the life of a mere mortal to one who believes she is a Goddess?

Fixing Vensa's gaze, I asked, "The cemetery, Vensa. Why the dead Mok-sa? Is that not a sacrilege to treat our comrades in such a way? Why do the malkops bring human dead to fertilize their fruit trees?"

She shrugged her beautiful shoulders. "It would be a sacrilege *not* to. We Mok-sa always allow our dead to fertilize what future generations shall need. This way they continue to serve our duty to expand across this planet. What difference does it make if they fertilize grain fields...or fertilize the malkops' trees? The fruit of those trees is all they eat, and the bodies of animals are mostly too large for them to carry, or too small to be worth the trouble. So Mok-sa bodies are best."

Vensa glanced away. "Get ready, daughters. More eggs are coming. Wade into the pool, you young ones."

They began to enter, some barely keeping their

heads above water.

Vensa looked back to Milo. "It is time for you to go. Milo, say goodbye to Bruna for you shall not see her again. She is safe here. She shall enjoy a long and productive life in the confines of my Sacred Spring."

I threw a stricken look at Bruna. She returned it with equal sadness. Her arms remained by her sides.

"You older ones, take him now. Bruna, accompany Milo to the palisade and command my warriors to make sure he is permitted to leave my city in peace, along with his property. Make sure none of the girls traffic with the boys. And you girls make sure Bruna also traffics with no one, including Milo, but that she returns here to me."

"Yes, Goddess," came the uniform reply from many youthful throats.

Turning to obey Vensa's command, I walked briefly away from the Sacred Spring and back toward the charnel pits, now escorted by six or eight girls, and a disconsolate Bruna. Suddenly I thought I saw furtive wings that were unlike those of the malkop-selks, which even now flew over my head carrying corpses, their lovely forms and faces having a most disturbing impact on my Little One within. I snapped my head toward the pool and glimpsed a flutter of translucent insect wings about a bulbous head that displayed a thousand eyes, green-scaled arms and legs attached to a dark-green body.

Anger—or was it panic—seized me and I took a step to return.

Four flint-tipped wooden spears contacted my skin, wielded by a half-dozen, hard-faced girls. I dared not proceed. The girls' flinty stares were as sharp as the tips of their spears and I was exhausted and weaponless. There would be no disobeying their Goddess.

"Atasan has come," one girl said matter-of-factly, making clear the thing's visitation to their Goddess was routine. As I watched, the green-scaled male malkop descended with all deliberateness to Vensa's Sacred Spring where what ensued I could not see as I was ushered into the charnel pits.

Past the pits, past the field of white spherical eggs, already expanding significantly as obedient young girls in unison brought more from Vensa's Sacred Spring, past the mid-chamber where the eggs were larger and becoming differentiated as older girls fed them, and finally past the magenta lozenges where the oldest and strongest girls, whom Vensa had declared would grow into adults and old age still tending to this task, carried more lozenges to the top of the tall altar for the malkops to retrieve. There were many more malkops than girls, I noted, as the cavern filled with wings.

What would they do if they can't get Mok-sa bodies? I wondered.

This became clear as I passed through the cavern and several malkops dropped the bodies of two young boys adorned with alien tattoos and strange insignia of some unknown animal that reminded me of wild cattle, boys with brutal injuries as if slain in battle.

So Vensa has already sent her young warriors against her wayward daughter Nesta who must have already established her own city, a city doubtless organized precisely as Vensa's City of Ven, with Nesta perhaps destined to enjoy as long a lifespan as Vensa Herself, a war between mother and daughter to last millennia.

All this flashed through my mind as we approached the palisade. The gate swung open with girls and boys mobbed in separate groups, each well-armed, each organized to prevent any physical trafficking between the two.

I looked at Bruna. "I still don't understand. How can Vensa mate with...*that thing?*"

She stared back. "I do not have all the answers either, Milo. But everything you've seen here is daily habit. And concerning us? I know She will not change her mind. So this is goodbye."

"What kind of world have we created, Bruna? This brand-new world of Mok-sa merged with hornets? A world forever without romance, without love? Only insect reproduction without limit."

"We can only hope, Milo, that someday, somehow, love will return."

"I shall hope with you."

Sighing, I stepped close and before the shocked crowd of eternally segregated youths could stop me, planted a swift kiss on Bruna's cheek: trafficking with the forbidden.

With that, the flinty spears intervened and pried us apart. Bruna returned to spend her life serving the City of Ven's Goddess; while they escorted me across the burgeoning settlement to the outermost gate where I was handed my rifle and two satchels, mine and Bruna's.

They motioned me in no mistaken terms to depart.

As I trudged back toward Ror, behind me wailed yet another Calling For Sons, as Vensa replenished her warriors with yet another dozen male infants just emerging from purple lozenges, who, in the fashion of all things on Maalstrom, I was confident would grow preternaturally into adult men ready to lay down their lives in constant war to expand the power of their City of Ven and their Sun-God Vensor.

Banned as they were from entering the sacred enclosure, the boys it seemed had switched their allegiance from a queen whom they had never seen to a male god whom they called *Vensor*, a god whom they in their ignorance of femaleness had already ascribed to Vensa's Temple of the Double Sun, a militant male god appropriate to an aggressive race of warriors whose only job was to feed and guard their god *Vensor's* Sacred Temple of the Double Sun.

Chapter 13

The way back was longer than I remembered. I had rushed, ignoring hunger and fatigue, but now as I traced my way back to my little settlement dubbed *Ror*, it seemed endless days passed. I had exhausted my food during the previous trip and I found myself increasingly famished, which made my progress even slower.

At length the Hedronmas River to my south, which my path paralleled, began its bend to the southeast, signaling I was close to home. Yet I could barely put one foot in front of the other. My white uniform, now torn and stained until almost unrecognizable, was so useless that I discarded what remained of it and wrapped tough elephant leaves around my torso, tied in place with the strap from my satchel which I threw away. I had another purpose in discarding the uniform: not possessing Mika's ability to locate nutrition from plants, I had resolved to satisfy my hunger in the most primitive manner by violating the most sacred taboo that our race had conceived of. I decided to kill and eat an innocent animal.

Were my values and morals falling away? I reminded myself that necessity knows no bounds, that survival comes first, that this was temporary, a one-time event that I would never repeat. But I had to fill my stomach. Hunger was driving out every other thought.

Unable to manage the final stretch to Ror, I watched and waited from the shelter of the forest bordering the vast plain. The hunger grew worse. Hardly able to stand, I relied on my new camouflage to cover what I intended to do, what I must do or perish.

At last, I was rewarded by the appearance of a herd of ungulates which, though new to me, seemed to present my best chance of securing sustenance. Quadrupeds, the largest grunted as it consumed the yellow-tan grass, sensing no danger. The larger ones were too imposing and their down-slung tusks too potentially lethal for me to tackle. Instead, I focused on the young ones intermixed with the adults.

I selected a calf suckling its mother, aimed my rifle, and unleashed a veritable barrage of ear-splitting loud gunshots, gambling to secure my meal at the same time that I frightened the herd into fleeing.

To my surprise and relief that is what happened.

A single calf dropped dead instantly, and the herd fled in panic until it was no longer visible on the horizon. And to my further surprise I had at the same time killed the mother, which dropped dead beside the calf.

After verifying that none of the creatures were any longer in sight, I ventured cautiously forth until I came upon the animals. Taking the short knife from Bruna's satchel, I swiftly, if clumsily, carved off a hind leg from the calf. Unwilling to postpone my nourishment any longer, I sparked a fire right in the open, cooked the entire leg, cut off a small portion, then forced a bite down my throat.

I wretched. My superego had not yet convinced my ego that meat was edible, that consuming it would save my life. I vomited. I forced down another bite...once more vomited.

I could not do it. My entire system revolted against this crime against Nature. With disgust, I spat out all that remained in my mouth and rinsed the last of it away with what remained of my water. I simply could not lower myself to the level of Khurko.

Khurko. I had forgotten him. For an entire week I had left him locked up in our impromptu jail without food or water, only a few roots and grains that I had tossed hastily in before I left. Was he still alive? Standing up, I made as if to throw the cooked leg in the bush. Then changed my mind. If Khurko still lived, the least I could do was to bring the cooked leg back to Ror and let him have it. The dead calf would remain dead in any event, it was too late to reverse that.

I felt sorry for Tau-3. Yes, he was a vile criminal but he was insane and was not responsible for his insanity. The leg may save his life as he certainly was by now near death inside his cell. I owed any Mok that much, even a murderous criminal Mok.

But now I was faced with my own imminent death. I could not eat the calf. Or the flesh of the mother. And I had not found sufficient roots and fruit to stay alive.

My eyes fell on the carcass of the mother which lay on one side next to the slaughtered calf. A man on the brink of starvation will try many strange things to remain alive, and I could think of only one, certainly the strangest of all.

Dropping to my knees, I stroked the mother's udders. I was both happy and revolted to discover the udders squirted rich milk. Thus, I relieved my hunger, stamping the objections of horrified Little Milo into the dirt as I suckled, life flowing back into me as I ingested the sweet liquid.

At last, I felt capable of travel. Shouldering the leg for Khurko and the rifle for myself, I plodded a ways toward Ror when a movement caught my eye.

I turned. On the open plain, several malkops flew upon what was left of the calf carcass and lifted it off the ground. This in itself was not surprising, knowing the habits of the beautiful creatures as I now did. Fully aware that they were always in the sky even if barely visible and were always waiting to retrieve the bodies of the dead, I now understood their purpose. They were only feeding their fungus fruit trees.

I was very surprised, though, to see that these malkops were not the larger variety that I was familiar with, and that I had seen in Ven, but were smaller and, to all appearances, weaker. I was even more surprised to see that they coveted a dead animal since all the malkops, as Vensa had said, concern themselves primarily with dead Mok-sa, their *siblings*.

The malkops seemed in a hurry to be off with their prize, ignoring the carcass of the mother which apparently was too heavy to lift. Tracing their flight with one hand shielding my brow, I watched them fly, not west, but southeast in the direction of Ror.

I fought the idea. Little Milo dismissed it with a smirk. I stabbed it with every blade my mind could conjure. But it refused to die. Lurching upright, I forced my feet to carry me back along the tree line, back toward Ror, where I felt the final answers must lie.

In less than an hour, I arrived at the rocky outcropping at the top of which stood our little barracks.

I paused.

Much as I felt sorry for Khurko, I had to investigate the destination of these new, stunted malkops. Or more precisely, I felt I knew already what, where, and why. I could not face Khurko, even a helpless half-starved Khurko, without first satisfying my curiosity. I had no reason to find joy in the barracks anyway now that no one was left there but him and me.

Tossing the leg at the foot of the stony slope, I circumvented the outcropping, and again following the line of the river, I soon arrived at the far side where our own spring, the Ror spring, spilled down in a series of noisy waterfalls to join the river Hedronmas.

Climbing the rocky incline, I followed the stream upward as I had often done, this time however not to retrieve water for myself and my co-wives, but to relieve my distress as to what I was certain I would find.

After splashing through the final rapid, I approached the cleft that defined a small shelter around a swiftly eddying pool, just the sort of pool and the sort of shelter that one might need if one were to wish to birth a new world.

Figures emerged immediately from the shadows—my eyes required moments to adjust—focused on three sharp sticks aimed at my midriff. The sticks were held by what I could only call small children. All males, as was apparent from their nudity, not even old enough to make loincloths for themselves. But their eyes displayed a harshness and purpose not seen in any child I had ever known. These creatures, as human in appearance as any Mok, could not have been more than a week old. Yet they walked. And no tattoos...yet.

Behind them stood three more children, this time female, again not having had time to weave cloth to hide their nudity. The girls stood at the back of the shelter, apprehensive and fearful.

I had little time to inspect this latest example of the new world, this new society that was coming into being on Maalstrom, a corruption of our own DNA, for in the pool itself sat the last of our women.

"Tlata," I mumbled.

She too was nude. Standing up to full height she looked at me and smiled the same old engaging smile as ever, and for several seconds I felt my old lust reawaken, her charms as magical as ever, her body as slender and appealing, not yet acquiring the obesity that endless reproduction would bring. At her feet in the swirling water lay a batch of a dozen eggs in different stages of development, from spherical and white to oval and darker. Along the rim and out of the water rested several gourds and torn lozenges alongside several male infants crying for nourishment since the male children had abandoned them for their sticks to defend their home from the intruder. The ovals squirmed, the female children having halted feeding time to stare at me in fear.

"Milo," answered Tlata, "I wondered how long it would take for you to visit. How long it would take before you missed me."

"I indeed have missed you." My eyes wandered about the little enclosure. On one side, almost stuffed in a corner, I noticed a small pile of corpses of small animals with a short altar next to them. I had no need to guess their purpose. The topmost corpse was that of a slain calf with a bullet hole through its skull; the very one I had just shot on the plain. In their midst had already sprouted a pale trunk with pale fruit at the top.

Stepping to the cleft, I looked up and noticed the same small malkops I had seen fluttering about outside, also fearful of approaching their altar with an intruder nearby. Too small to fly to Klopus for human corpses, they were collecting whatever roadkill they could find to nourish their only source of food, the fungus trees.

I knew all this would change, of course. Tlata's City of Ror would grow as rapidly as Vensa's City of Ven, just as Tumsa and Nasveta had doubtless established cities of their own across the plain. And, as I finally guessed, as Vedega Alpha-1, our missing commander must already have established hers.

My head spun with the whirlwind.

"Tlata. How could this happen? How could our rational world, our advanced science, collapse into a primitive society where the only thing that matters is endless reproduction? How can you participate?"

She shook her head, as puzzled as I. "What do you mean, Milo? How can you ask me why I take care of my children? Why I should love *all* my children? Don't all mothers?"

"Of course, But these are no children such as I have ever seen."

"No, thank Atasan. They are independent almost from birth. They do not need constant supervision like our old Mok-sa children who took over twenty Earth years to grow and to learn all that science that you worship so much." She looked lovingly at her offspring. "These children, who I am so lucky to have, use every waking moment caring for me rather than the other way around. What mother would not prefer these over the other?"

"But in this new world, Tlata, there will be no

science, no learning, no progress. Your world will be static. And the children that you and the other queens produce will soon drown Maalstrom in their numbers, flooding the planet, fighting each other in a forever war for resources and space. Can't you see that?"

"Other queens?" She lost her smile, and a hard look took hold. *"Competitors,* you mean. My soldiers will fight...and they will win."

"Or lose," I added. "Which, knowing what I know, will mean your death as well as theirs."

Tlata shrugged. "There are other springs, other places for an exiled mother to take refuge in."

I hesitated to mention what else I knew, that once her new generative ability kicked in, Tlata herself would become too large to stand unaided, much less to flee. And that Vensa was too close, too murderous, and already too powerful for any colony in close-by Ror to compete with her.

Glancing at my booted feet, I tried to ignore my leafy loincloth and her nudity, which had triggered my passion. Looking up I said, "Tell me something, Tlata. Were you ever stung by the leroo? It could have been painless, so small that perhaps you never noticed it."

Slowly she shook her head. "I know what you suspect. You often asked us women if we were stung back in Klopus. No, Milo. Not then, and not since. I would know if I had." Her eyes fell over her exquisite body and she examined every precious limb, exciting me and Little Milo until we almost burst our leafy bower.

I continued, "And Bruna was definitely stung...yet only she is *not* pregnant. Could it be that I am wrong in all I've thought? Could it be that the sting of the leroo is not the source of the contamination?"

"Contamination." She laughed, her breasts calling to me with their shaking. "Relief, rather. Relief from the suffocating control of our former world, from the endless rules and indoctrination, from all the can'ts and shouldn'ts." She shook her head. "I won't do that again. I won't go back. Here..." she gazed about her new little world, "here, I am free. Such complete freedom that I would die a hundred times before I give this up."

"So there is nothing more to say."

She angled her head. Puzzled but serene.

"Except..." I turned away, then back. "Except goodbye. My love."

Again her smile. Happy again. "My love."

With that, I exited, to the visible relief not only of the three almost toddlers who let their spears relax and of the three little girls whose fears eased, and of the several small malkops who promptly flew back into the cleft where I got a closer look as they went in. The malkops were nearly infants themselves, still no loincloths on their nude bodies that were obviously female but devoid of the physical development of mature malkops.

Yet mature malkops were also near, riding updrafts in the air, eyeing me as if fearing I may harm their little selk sisters. I realized they might be watching the rifle, so I shouldered it firmly to show that I had no intention of using it if by chance they understood what it was.

Down the slope I caught another flutter in the air. Looking at the source, my gaze leveled on what I had regarded as the ultimate evil, the chief author of the destruction of our Mok-sa society, the insect-eyed drone of what I knew now was not an alien species at all, but—somehow—*us*. Somehow, of us, out of us. The thing that Vensa's girls had called *Atasan*, the name that Tlata had also just used, thanking her own god.

Having visited Vensa, the *thing* ceased its dragonfly hovering and plummeted to the cleft now to visit Tlata. Without a glance in my direction, it entered without resistance.

Backtracking, I followed the path around the Ror outcrop until I came again to the footfall of the stony hill where a gentle slope led up to our barrack. The severed leg of meat still lay where I had tossed it. Sighing, and against my better judgment, I picked it up. Shaking hungry insects off, I swung it under one arm and climbed up the slope to give it to Khurko. I could not help it. I felt sorry for him. Maybe I would find he had recovered his sanity. Maybe he would thank me. Maybe I would open his cell and he would be appreciative and shake my hand and happily embrace me and I would no longer be a Robinson Crusoe but would have a loyal Friday to help me pass the time, help me ward off my loneliness now that I could no longer see any of my former paramours. Indeed, I would need help to find a new place to live since Tlata's little colony would soon grow into a city whose warriors would certainly chase me out and force me to find another refuge.

If only I could understand it all. If only the last pieces would fall into place. Hornets, Atasan, one week old warriors, lozenges placed on altars, bricks made of spit, winged *selks* as alluring as my own former wives...they swam in my brain looking for holes to fill.

I approached the door, the labors of the short Maalstrom day fatiguing me as the light already began to fade.

The door stood ajar.

I was sure I had left it closed. Perhaps one of Tlata's little minions had tinkered with it. Perhaps Tlata herself.

Entering, I thought I glimpsed a shadow cross the hallway at its far end. Given the darkness following the sunlit outside, I could not be certain. I gave in to my pity, my yearning to help another Mok-sa, every other human anywhere who was in need, and trudging the length of the corridor as I was once more growing tired from lack of food. Or was it my own reluctance coming to the fore, my feeling of revulsion for having to once again look upon the face of insanity? At any rate, I exited the corridor and passed through the small room on the left that gave onto the equally small room that housed our little jail.

Sunlight streamed in from an upper unrepaired rafter and threw its glare over the stout wooden bars that contained Khurko. For a moment the interior of the cell was bathed in darkness, then my eyes adjusted and I no longer feared that my inmate had escaped. From the interior shadow he loomed and cautiously gripped the bars. Khurko was still there, still imprisoned, still alive, though I had expected him to be on the verge of starvation, and thinner.

The same old glare of hatred, contempt, and madness blazed forth from his visage. His round-rimmed eyes seemed to jump out of their sockets and stab me with their pain. His hands were dirtier than before, but I could not help but notice that his white uniform with the Tau-3 sign in Greek letters remained barely soiled, almost as clean as the day we arrived.

"So, you still live," I uttered beneath my breath. Had I been hoping that I would find only a corpse? I exhaled. "That is good," I lied. I swung the scorched animal leg before him. For the first time I thought his insanity faded as his eyes focused on the meat like a tiger on a slab of raw flesh. His stare shifted back to me.

"Step away from the bars, Khurko, and I will give this meat to you to relieve your hunger and keep you from starvation."

He stepped back and I slid the leg through two of the bars.

I had expected him to leap upon the flesh like the tiger of my imagination, eager to relieve his famished body, but he casually picked it up and only slowly tore off small bites of meat, which he chewed in what seemed an inordinately long time before swallowing, all the while keeping his angry eyes upon me.

"Khurko. I don't expect you to have any gratitude for my kindness, but cannot you find it in yourself to come to your senses? Think, Khurko. Think how far you have fallen. From a rational human at one with nature, inner and outer, the pride of our civilization in you, you have chosen to throw it all aside and embrace what our ancestors fought so hard against for so long. You have embraced the primitive within. You have returned to the state of an animal, the most despised of creatures. And even celebrated it. Can you not see this? Fight it, Khurko, fight it. It is not too late. It is never too late to embrace sanity and civilization and rejoin the community of your peers."

My gaze dropped. "I mean, our erstwhile community. Assuming anything still remains in Klopus, or anyone there still remains alive." I returned his stare again. "But whether our comrades live or not, it is still imperative that we ourselves remain civilized. By, for instance, bathing, shaving every day, repairing our home, cooking our food...and refraining from the eating of our comrades, both human and animal. Yes, I know you have become a cannibal," I chided.

He responded by tearing off a larger chunk of flesh and consuming it with more relish.

Having received no utterance from Khurko other than guttural growls as he ate his meal, I gave up and turned away. It weighed on me like a mountain that he was no better than when I had left. It was after all only my own desperation and loneliness that had brought me here. Far better that I had let him die in his cell.

A crack as of dropped crockery rang out.

Temple of the Double Sun

Barely able to overcome my depression I turned, only slowly, and in a single moment I glimpsed wooden bars clatter to the floor, the wooden trellis that had housed them having long been cut or eroded by some tool. Khurko loomed large before me, free of his cage.

His fist flashed briefly in the air—smote my face with the strength of solid muscle.

"Raag!" his voice finally erupted, as in triumph.

The other fist raised—struck me again—sent me folding beneath it, collapsing.

Trying to stand, I could not. Only roll to stare up at him.

His eyes had no trace of reason, his pupils piercing me with their shafts of anger, madness flaming as from the depths of perdition. Satisfied that his victim could no longer resist, he straightened.

I was not certain he even recognized me or had understood a single word I had said. A cloud of madness seemed to float about his head, and he turned and wandered about for a moment. Then some idea seemed to surface, and he spun and hurried out the side door that led out of the barrack.

It took me a few seconds to sit up, a few moments more to stand.

Then it hit me: perhaps Khurko was not quite

so insane after all. The barrack side door led to the rover.

At once I launched to my feet and raced outside after him, losing what was left of my leafy loincloth in the process, a nude animal of civilization pursuing a clothed man who had reverted to predator.

Racing along the stony path, I burst upon the small cavity where we had left the rover, the slight elevation protecting it from being dislodged by the wind. As I threw myself forward, the side door slammed shut and I saw his figure leap behind the controls.

The rover lurched upward. I hurled myself pell-mell upon a landing strut and clung with the crook of one elbow.

Up the rover sped.

The lurch of its impetus threatened to tear my arm away — gusts battered my exposed face.

In but a moment, the rover changed direction. Suddenly it launched toward the Hedronmas, crossed it in seconds, then turned northeast, toward Klopus.

Unwilling to suffer the fate of the engineer who had found himself in the same predicament, I frantically pulled myself higher, and as the vehicle's speed was not yet great, managed to grip the handle of the side door. Swinging my body over the strut, I yanked the door wide and clambered within.

At the controls, Khurko turned his head and glared at me in alarm. Rising from the pilot's seat, in doing so he twisted the steering; he next punched the autopilot on the control panel, then leaped at me with a guttural cry.

I managed to survive his first assault by pushing him off with my feet.

He returned and sought to pummel me as before, his fists flinging right and left, but ignoring his blows, I found my feet, and standing, I blocked and ducked every punch until I was able to deliver several of my own.

The rover was climbing. I wondered how much farther it could carry us, how much power remained in its cells, the concern of Yezd. Then it lurched and sped on an even path. The jerk threw Khurko off balance.

Taking advantage in what had been an even fight between two famine-stricken men, I used my last energy to pound his cheek.

Khurko collapsed, an empty sack.

The grinding of gears alerted me to the danger of plummeting, and I staggered to the controls where I discovered Khurko had cracked the autopilot. I could not change our course. Try as I did, I could not swerve the ailerons up or down, the rudder left or right. Wherever we were headed, it would be one-way, and directly south where our last survey had sighted nothing but ocean.

The intervening land raced beneath us. Returning to Khurko, I ensured he lay inert on the floor, and as before I secured him to the inside of the side door with a spare strap from the rover's interior.

I again examined our course.

We sped across unknown territory, high ridges visible in the distance. In minutes we passed over the ridges, and before long the southern ocean swelled beneath us, stretching to the horizon.

I still could not influence our direction, the damned autopilot resisted every jammed finger and object that I applied. There was nothing to do but wait, wait for our journey to end, for the energy to finally falter, condemning an unlikely pair to suffer an unlikely death on an unlikelier world.

An hour over the water, with land now but a memory, Khurko groaned. Turning slowly over, he sat up, saw the strap binding him. He bit it. Far from trying to free himself, however, I saw that he was attempting to tear off portions to eat. As he had neglected to bring his calf leg, I had nothing to give him except remnants of tuber in a small gourd that had been overlooked and left in the rover from our previous attempt to get airborne.

I hungrily ate most; threw the last scrap at him. He snapped it up, swallowed the last of it, then tried to eat the gourd. Unable to, he returned to gnawing his strap.

For some time the gears behaved. Now I heard more creaking and grinding. Then it again ceased. How long did we have? Funny how when one's last moments approach, one attempts to calculate not just the remaining seconds, but the remaining milliseconds, anything to keep savoring the sweetness of life, even life in the company of a carnivorous madman in a vehicle about to take the final descent to a watery grave.

Unable to alter our course, after perhaps an hour at the controls, I gave up and lay back into a half-sleep. I had no choice. No food means no energy. No energy dictates sleep. I knew the danger with Khurko at my back, but a higher authority took command.

I slept.

Chapter 14

For how long I slept, I could not know. Minutes, hours, days perhaps. When I regained consciousness, the meager rations I had consumed at last enabling me to reopen my eyes, I found Khurko had sunk into the same unconsciousness, breathing feebly, but breathing.

I blinked. Unable to believe it, I blinked again. On the horizon a belt of green had appeared. As our little rover sped through the atmosphere of Maalstrom's tropics, the belt enlarged and finally revealed a woodland with a stretch of yellow beach at its feet.

The rover jerked. With a sickening lurch it dropped and a glance at the controls showed that its power supply, which had bordered on exhausted since we left Ror, flashed red. Out. Unbelievably, the gears had held throughout our trip, my little repair job having kept them in line. But now they too began to creak and the ailerons and rudder went haywire. Before I knew it, the rover began to spiral down, though, thank Teknos, ever closer to that distant mirage of yellow and green.

A dreg of energy found its way to the engine and neutralizer and the vehicle once more sped forward, then aimed almost vertically down, and in another moment or two I managed to level the ailerons so that we skipped once upon the waves, twice, then settled into the surf fifty yards from the blue-washed sand.

As fast as I could manage, which I don't mind confessing was slow compared to any person of normal condition, I slid open the side door and untied a still unconscious Khurko from the strut and pulled him into the water with me.

The water was not deep and I found I could stand, although with some difficulty given the constant waves. Slogging forward and dragging Khurko behind, I pushed the remaining fifty meters until we gained the shore where I fell at once to my knees and praised all the gods including Teknos—and I again don't mind confessing—even the new god Vensor, where a glance at the sky showed the double sun still slowly merging, signaling the onset of cooler weather. I at least was still on Maalstrom, laying to rest Little Milo's hysterical fear on that account.

Khurko moaned.

Why did I bother with him? I cannot honestly explain that even to myself. I suppose Robinson felt the same whenever Friday fell into trouble. Mad and lethal he may be, but he was still human, still one of us. And I still did not want to be alone even if the company of a madman was almost like being alone.

Despite all, I was not yet ready to give up. Not ready to lay down and let vultures peck my eyes, or whatever may pass for vultures on this planet given that I had not yet seen such, having absolved the malkop-selks of that sin.

In the shallows, sizable fish swam. Quite close in fact. I recalled how the fish in the Hedronmas had been easy to catch, not having been exposed to hunting by anything on two legs. When a ghost of energy returned to me, I decided to try my luck.

Though nude, I still had my boots, now so waterlogged as to be useless. I extracted the laces and bent one of the eyelets into a hook. Approaching the stunted trees that lined the beach, I noticed that we had landed in another swamp with shallow pools and marsh stretching inland. Braving more clouds of gnats that stirred with each step, I began searching for something to serve as a fishing rod. I perceived that the pools also had fish. What could be easier?

Moving gradually into the nearest pool, I soon snatched a pair of decent-sized fish with my bare hands and tossed the laces and hook away as unnecessary. In moments, I had struck a fire and thoroughly cooked the fish before eating slices of them after removing the bones.

I lay with my back against a tree and promptly fell again into a coma.

Again, I have no idea how long I slept but when I awoke I felt indescribably refreshed, for the first time in what seemed an age ready to take on a day's labor.

Returning to Khurko, I confirmed that he still breathed. But I was not quite ready to thrust fish-flesh down his throat. I was not ready for him to be as alert and strengthened as I. Instead, I found myself so afflicted with the clouds of gnats that I was compelled to constantly swat them away. Glancing down, I discovered a red patch on one limb. This was a surprise. I did not recall the gnats at the swamp by Klopus as being such pests.

As my hunger was also already returning, I decided to return to the rover before it sank into mud and to retrieve what little was there. In a half hour or so I completed my trip, bringing back another satchel, though empty, and an assortment of tools and a knife, including—at the last moment—the glass viewer Yezd had used to amplify the landscape.

After snatching and cooking another fish, I cleaned and polished the viewer, and more as a lark than anything, focused the viewer on the annoying red patch.

What I saw was more than disturbing. Beneath the viewer I watched innumerable small gnats, which as I learned to my alarm were not any gnats with which I was familiar, but some distant kin. The insects had not only stingers of their own but had implanted them in my skin. I rubbed, I peeled but found them impossible to dislodge as they worked their way inside.

An idea came to me. Moving the viewer to other parts of my body I discovered similar patches everywhere, patches that could only have been inflicted before the rover had crashed. Say, in the swamp by Klopus, the swamp where we had first landed. For what seemed an eternity I sat beneath that tree with the double suns of tropical Maalstrom shining above, my mind doing acrobatics.

Could it be that something other than hornets—or, more precisely, something before our exposure to hornets—had already broken our DNA? Something that we had encountered the first day we arrived, within the first few minutes? Something that had damaged us in such a way that contamination by the leroo hornets thus became possible?

There was no doubt that we had merged with

the hornets. And that we had not merged with gnats. Assuming our DNA had been damaged, exposed, laid bare so to speak, by the initial encounter in the swamp, and given that it clearly was not the sting of the hornets that had caused the merging, since only our women who had *not* been stung were the ones giving birth to eggs, how then had we merged with the leroo-sa?

It may have been simple, something overlooked at the time, even accidental. My mind flipped through an array of incidents when I had first met the insects.

My mind paused, snagged on a seeming trivial memory. In the course of constructing the barracks on the very first day after our arrival, I had cleaned the new commons eating room. One of the insects that I swatted and discarded was a leroo hornet. Thinking nothing of it, I had tossed the thing into the trash...however, alongside the trash receptacle, the engineers had placed our new water container filled with our communal water, with no cover on top.

Might I have...could my aim have been just a little off? A single half-dead wasp dropping into our communal water?

I shook my head. Such was completely impossible. That alone simply could not have been the cause of all that had happened. But what if one consumed something still living and *very close in time* after one's DNA had been laid bare by the gnats...

I stood. There was one way to find out.

I hesitated. Could I live with the result? I had no choice but to try, my ecologist soul thirsted for truth. If exposed DNA followed quickly by drinking water that contained elements of a still living wasp could launch a dozen half-insect, half-human cities...

Earlier I had dragged Khurko under another tree and fed him a few bites of cooked fish. Now I returned to him, and stripping off his boots and now well-soiled uniform, I inspected his skin. He too was covered with pale red patches. The gnats had done whatever they were going to do and the patches were fresh.

Now was the time.

Khurko began to wake. Still too feeble to resist, he merely growled when I pulled him up and half-dragged, half-pushed him until we came to a more densely wooded grove away from the swamp where the gnats would no longer bother us.

Standing him against a young tree, I used the knife to cut a length of vine and I tied him to the trunk. I pulled down several of its branches and picked fruit from its stalks. For a last moment, I paused to utter the time-honored formula so the gods would bless my plan with success: "May it be good, fortunate, propitious." I suppressed the thought that nothing useful had resulted from Vedega's prior calling on the gods.

Then, with little effort on my part, since Khurko cooperated, I fed the raw fruit to him. He at once consumed it, willing to eat anything to stave off starvation.

I sat and waited.

What would the morrow bring? The final answer to all my questions? Or more puzzles without answers?

For hours I waited.

Then a day.

Then another day.

Disconsolate, I returned to the network of pools and caught another fish and made certain I thoroughly cooked it before eating it. I returned to Khurko and fed him more fruit from the tree. I slept beneath the shade of the quiet grove and watched the suns as they completed their merging, signaling the full arrival of what passed as winter on this strange planet, though, as I had been transported close to the equator, it had little effect locally.

A week passed and I lost faith in my quest, and my hypothesis on what had happened to my Moksa, on every explanation that my bedeviled mind had invented in my desperation as an ecologist to somehow finally explain my predicament, to understand what this planet had worked on us.

Returning to Khurko again and again, I inspected him for what I had hoped to find, and again and again I saw nothing, just a half-starved pathetic victim of madness...both his own and mine?

As the days passed, I grew stronger while Khurko grew weaker, despite the fruit that I repeatedly forced down his revolting throat. This had to work. My life's terminus could not end in such complete, such ignominious failure.

I gave up.

Trodding the sandy beach through the scattered pools and back to his little grove of trees, I decided to let my fantasies go and put an end to Khurko's pitiful life, at last to let him pass into the great unknown where I hoped soon to follow rather than continue to suffer so hopeless and distant an exile for the rest of what could only be a short lonely life.

Stepping beside him, I looked at his face.

He opened his eyes, and he seemed to understand what I planned. Some small remnant of sanity must have resided somewhere in those orbs as I glimpsed deep inside him a flash of fear.

I took out my knife and cut the vines that had kept him tied to the tree for weeks. Turning, I stepped away, prepared to complete the deed. Who am I kidding? I turned so he could seize the knife and finish *me*, leaving him to die of loneliness in my place.

He did not move.

I waited, hoping he would grab the knife and do what I had not the courage to do. I stared at the sky. He *must* do it. *Must* put me out of my misery.

Still, he did not come.

At last, I turned round to see if he had perhaps died at the very moment of his freedom. I saw him continue to stand where I had left him, remaining beside the tree as if frozen in place.

Looking down I noticed yet another of those twists that this alien planet always seems to have in store for the unwary. His feet had formerly been layered with sand and dirt, but now there was more: a brown roughness had appeared, a crusty patina that traveled both up his shins and downward into the dirt. Khurko himself was staring at his feet, and I saw that he was attempting to move them but failing.

An emotion rose within me, unsuspected in its power.

Rushing close, I shook Khurko, attempting to free him, to *make* him walk. He looked at me with terror in his eyes. He could not. Struggle though he might, his legs were locked in the soil.

My face broke into glee—I crowed aloud.

Khurko would never walk again but would stand forevermore where I had placed him.

My hypothesis had worked!

Khurko growled more deeply, and I suddenly noticed that he was far from the famished near-skeleton whom I had tied to the tree two weeks earlier. He was nourished, and certainly not from the few fruits that I had fed him, but from some other source. Even as I gazed at him, his muscles seemed to gain tone and grow. His face became fuller. The glow of madness in his eyes did not abate but also seemed to grow.

For a moment I felt my pity for him return. Knowing he could no longer follow me, I went to the nearest pool to fetch water for him to drink.

When I returned, I halted and my jaw opened. Khurko was eating something, something that dripped red. Coming closer, I discovered he had grabbed some small animal like a wood squirrel and was consuming it ravenously, his arms bulging with strength.

No, his madness had not departed. Would never depart.

It was then I noticed more: a sprinkling of saplings growing rapidly about him, each like the other, but all unlike every other sapling in the vicinity. These saplings bore at their top what appeared to be hair...human-like hair with bare flesh beneath it, human-like flesh. They grew as steadily as Khurko's legs were coming to resemble tree bark, as steadily as his feet became roots sunk deep into the ground. I had not planned on this. If the saplings were what I suspected, Khurko would never be lonely but was destined to enjoy the company of many companions, rooted like him. Perhaps exact duplicates...and just as mad? Only a distant future could tell.

A future I could not wait for.

At last, I had untied the knot. Clearly, the gnats that infest the swamps on Maalstrom broke the DNA code of us colonists by injection of their poisons. Once broken, any live DNA that we happened to ingest soon afterward must fuse with our DNA. In the case of my Mok-sa, a half-dead leroo hornet that I had negligently tossed into our water supply on the first day had transformed us into a unique fusion of human with hornet. In the case of Khurko, a deliberately induced pollinating tree fruit has, *is*, transforming him into a hybrid of human and tree that was already spreading by means of his unique half-human pollen, an unfortunate possibility that I had not expected when I performed my little experiment. I was only glad that I had cooked our fish so thoroughly, both mine and Khurko's. Otherwise, who knew what other bizarre fusion might have resulted?

I still did not have all the answers. But my mind spun with wild speculation. Could the sting of the leroo in fact be a prophylactic, somehow reversing the ecological effect that my accident had caused, limiting the population explosion of our new hybrid humanity? And could I be mistaken about Atasan, as I had been mistaken about everything else on this new world?

Now it was too late. Too late to reverse anything. Too late to regret my poor aim on that luckless day long ago when I inadvertently tossed a half-dead hornet into our water vat instead of into our trashcan. Too late to reverse what was happening to Khurko. Even too late for answers.

But not too late for me.

Far above I thought I glimpsed a familiar tell-tale dot. Could they be...do I dare hope that they could have come this far?

Plodding back to the beach, I trudged through the surf to the rover. Starting it up one last time, I gave it a final set of instructions and leapt out. Would its power be sufficient for one last charge to the gravity neutralizer?

Slugging away, I turned and watched the rover shake, jerk, then lurch free of the water. With barely a pause, it rose directly up, rising higher and higher until finally it was lost to my sight, heading for an orbit to last eons. Too tired, too depressed, but also too elated to think of anything clever, I had scribbled across the control panel: "bring bug spray". Let future colonists puzzle that out as I had puzzled out this mysterious planet.

I had but one last task to perform. My task alone, for me alone, all my duties either fallen away or bungled beyond repair.

Walking at least a half-hour to be far away from Khurko and his insane progeny, but not so far as to risk ingesting the wrong item now that I too was primed by the gnats for imminent fusion with some scrap of living DNA, I at last found what I wished: a wide grove of old-growth trees on a moderately lofty plateau, the trees spaced well apart so as not to interfere with visitors. Trees that were giving fruit.

Approaching several smaller ones, I pulled their branches down and with deliberateness— slowly, but with eagerness—ate their fruit.

The deed was done.

I sat at the edge of this blessed little wood, gazing down on the distant beach. Was I on an island, or had the rover brought us to an extension of the mainland? I neither knew nor cared. The clouds above dissolved from their prior portrayals of angry gods and transformed into smiling images such as those the blessed in paradise see.

It was not long in coming. Perhaps my longing,

and not only mine but of Little Milo, hurried the process, and in only a week while I consumed more and more of the fruit of Heaven's orchard, I felt the first changes in my feet. I dragged their heaviness to the precise location I desired...where The Visitors would see me.

There I stood. Fatigue vanished. Pain was gone. Hunger disappeared as my lower legs gradually changed into roots and sucked nutrition and energy from the Maalstrom earth itself. My body no longer felt cold or heat. I no longer ate or passed waste. I simply existed, feeling the wind and the sun on the skin of my body, which remained as human as before, nude as the day I was born, indeed reborn. Reborn into paradise where I raised my face to sing, to sing for my paramours, to attract and entice them.

At length...and who can tell how time passes for something that is part tree and part human? Was it a day? Or a century? Time has come to mean precisely nothing to me. I await only my eternal reward.

And on a moonlit night—the lurid shadows cast by Maalstrom's green moon enwrapping the soughing grove in its gorgeous embrace—one of Heaven's angels appeared. Out of the sky came one of its holy denizens. Her perfect face and beautiful eyes crowned by flowing blond hair and framed by wide wings found me standing beside the trees, and she spiraled down to see this new addition to the populace of Heaven.

Alighting before me, she stepped close and her eyes locked with mine. My love for her exuded from every pore of my being and my arms slowly lifted and spread wide to invite. With a crinkled and happy smile, the selk stepped closer, pressed her full breasts against my naked chest, sealed her lips with mine and with a deep sigh raised her loincloth and slid onto my erect member.

My happiness was complete.

Thus my days and nights would pass while I perfected my singsong to attract as many selks as I could while they flew on their mysterious errands. Perhaps my lifespan, too, stretching into millennia while all around me my saplings were already appearing, saplings with human-like hair on top, bare human skin beneath, and roots at the bottom. A forest of Little Milos were on the way in this, our own little paradise, a paradise such as the Chaldeans of Earth never dreamed.

Glenn Lazar Roberts

Glenn Lazar Roberts is an international attorney and writer of sci-fi, horror, satire, and adventure fantasy novels. Glenn has taught college, professionally translated Arabic and Russian, and credits an eclectic group of famous writers for inspiring him to write, including Jack Vance, Robert E. Howard, Edgar Rice Burroughs, Mervyn Peake, H.P. Lovecraft, Ray Bradbury, Arthur C. Clarke, Isaac Asimov, and H.G. Wells, among many other Masters of the Art. "I love language. I am perpetually afloat on a sea of script." Roberts has edited the work of other aspiring writers and hosts a writing critique circle. When he's not writing he enjoys swimming. He lives in Houston with his wife and kids.

Glenn Lazar Roberts

Enjoy more novels and short stories from

 **PRESS**

https://www.twbpress.com

Science Fiction, Supernatural, Horror, Urban Fantasy, Thrillers, Romance, and more